THE SECRET OF THE GLEN

Leona stood before the Duke of Ardness, well aware that her whole body was trembling.

"I understand that you rode off my land today," the Duke began slowly. Although he was speaking in a controlled, almost unemotional voice, Leona could feel the anger vibrating from him.

"You wished to visit Lord Strathcairn? I suppose you imagine you are in love with him?"

Leona did not answer and after a moment the Duke said:

"I presume he has told you about his wife?"

"His ... wife?"

Leona could hardly whisper the words. She was sure she was about to faint ...

BARBARA CARTLAND

Bantam Books by Barbara Cartland
Ask your bookseller for the books you have missed

Barbara Cartland
The Secret of the Glen

BANTAM BOOKS · TORONTO · NEW YORK · LONDON

THE SECRET OF THE GLEN
A Bantam Book | November 1976

ISBN 0–553–02950–9

Published simultaneously in the United States and Canada

Bantam Books are published by Bantam Books, Inc. Its trade-
mark, consisting of the words "Bantam Books" and the por-
trayal of a bantam, is registered in the United States Patent
Office and in other countries. Marca Registrada. Bantam
Books, Inc., 666 Fifth Avenue, New York, New York 10019.

PRINTED IN THE UNITED STATES OF AMERICA

Author's Note

The cruelty of Highland Clansmen will never be forgotten or forgiven.

So that they might lease their Glens and braes to sheepfarmers from the Lowlands and the English, the Chieftains cleared the crofts of men, women, and children, using police and soldiers if necessary.

Starting in 1785 in Sutherland, the last eviction took place in 1854 in Ross-shire. Hundreds of thousands of Scots were forced to emigrate, a third to starve or die of cholera, typhoid, or smallpox in the stinking holds of rotten ships. In 1831, 58,000 people left Britain for Canada, and 66,000 left the following year.

At the beginning of the Crimean War, the English turned instinctively to the Highlands for their superb fighting men. Between 1793 and 1815, 72,385 Highlanders had carried Wellington's armies to victory against Napoleon.

But in 1854 the recruiting officers were met with bleats and barks. A spokesman told the Landlords:

"Send your deer, your roes, your lambs, dogs, shepherds, and gamekeepers to fight the Russians, they have done us no harm!"

The hills and moors of the north are empty of those who once made glorious the history of Scotland, and the tartan is their shroud.

Chapter One

1850

Leona felt the wind whistling through every crack and corner of the carriage even though it was strongly and expensively made.

In fact, the gale blowing across the moors was so strong that the horses could only move at a snail's pace.

It was disappointing, she thought, because the previous day had been bright with sunshine and she had sat staring out onto the purple moorlands.

She had been entranced by the high peaks silhouetted against the sky and had felt a child-like excitement when she saw silver cascades pouring down into the burns.

"It is even more beautiful than Mama described it," she told herself, and knew that nothing could be more thrilling than to be in Scotland.

Ever since she had been a baby Leona had listened to the stories of Scottish bravery, of the feuds of the Clans, and of the loyalty of the Jacobites to the "King across the water."

The stories had been more than mere tales of heroism.

To her mother they were so real, so poignant, and filled with so much nostalgia that her voice as she related them had throbbed with emotions which her daughter could never forget.

1

To Elizabeth Macdonald, the treachery of the Campbells at the massacre of Glencoe was an event that might have happened yesterday.

Although she lived away from her native land, to her dying day she remained a Scot in thought, word, and deed.

"Your mother looks upon me as a mere Sassenach, however much she loves me," her father would sometimes say to Leona with a smile on his lips.

But he was right in saying that his wife loved him.

Leona could not imagine that any two people could have been happier together than her mother and father.

They were desperately poor, but that did not matter.

When Richard Grenville was invalided out of the Army he had only his pension and a crumbling Manor House in Essex on which to support his wife and their only child.

He had farmed in a dilatory, half-hearted manner which supplied them with chickens and eggs, with ducks and turkeys, and even sometimes with mutton.

It never seemed to matter that there was not enough actual money with which to buy elegant clothes or smart carriages, or to pay for visits to London.

What was important was that they were together.

Leona thought that her home was always full of sunshine and laughter, despite the fact that the covers on the furniture were thread-bare and it was difficult to guess how the curtains had looked before they faded.

"We were happy . . . so very happy," she told herself now, "until Papa died."

Richard Grenville had died unexpectedly of a heart-attack and his wife had no wish to go on living without him.

She had gone into a despondent decline from which not even Leona could arouse her.

"Come and look at the baby chickens, Mama," she would beg, or she would ask her mother to help her exercise the two horses which were their only mode of conveyance.

But Mrs. Grenville had just let her life ebb away as she sat about the house lost in her memories and only counting the days until she could be reunited with her husband.

It was very much as an afterthought that her mother had made any plans for her.

"You must not die, Mama," Leona had said frantically one evening.

She could almost see her mother slipping into the unseen world where she was convinced her husband was waiting for her.

Her words seemed to have no impact and she had added despairingly:

"What will become of me? What shall I do, Mama, if you leave me?"

It was as if the problem had presented itself to Elizabeth Grenville for the first time.

"You cannot stay here, darling."

"Not alone," Leona agreed. "Besides, when you die there will not even be your widow's pension to support me."

Mrs. Grenville closed her eyes as if the word "widow" hurt her. Then she said:

"Bring me my writing materials."

"Who are you going to write to, Mama?" Leona asked curiously as she obeyed.

She knew they had few relations. Her father's parents came from Devonshire and were long since dead.

Her mother had been born near Loch Leven, but she had become an orphan before she married and had lived with an aged Aunt and Uncle, who had died a few years after she came south.

There must be cousins belonging to both her parents, Leona thought, but she had never met them.

"I am writing," Elizabeth Grenville said in her

soft voice, "to someone who was my closest friend when I was a girl."

Leona waited, wondering what her mother would tell her.

"Jeannie McLeod and I were almost brought up together," she said, "and because my parents were dead I spent months of every year in her home, while occasionally she came to mine."

Her eyes were full of memories as she went on:

"It was Jeannie's parents who introduced me to Society at the Balls in Edinburgh when we were both nearly eighteen, and when I left Scotland with your father the only thing I regretted was that I must leave Jeannie behind."

"You have not seen her since, Mama?"

"We used to write to each other regularly," Mrs. Grenville replied, "but then, you know how it is, Leona, one always puts off until tomorrow what one should do today."

She sighed before she continued:

"I always received a very sweet letter from her at Christmas, except, now that I think of it, no letter came last year."

She paused. Then she said:

"It may have . . . I was so . . . distraught at losing your . . . father that I can remember very little about Christmas."

"That is not surprising; it was a very miserable time, Mama," Leona agreed.

Her father had died in the middle of December and there had been no Christmas-tree, no presents, and because she thought it would upset her mother Leona had not even allowed the carol-singers to come to the house.

"I am writing to Jeannie now," Mrs. Grenville said, "to beg her to look after you when I am gone, and to love you as we loved each other when we were girls together."

"Do not talk of leaving me, Mama," Leona begged. "I want you to get well. I want you to stay with me and help me look after the house and the farm."

Her mother did not reply and after a moment Leona said:

"It was what Papa would have wished, as you well know. He would have hated to see you as you are now."

"It is no use, dearest," her mother answered. "When your father left us he took my heart and my soul with him. There is nothing in me now but an aching, longing need to find him and for us to be together again."

Hearing the pain in her mother's voice, Leona knew there was nothing more she could say.

She watched her mother write the letter and only when she saw to whom it was addressed did she give an exclamation of surprise.

"The Duchess of Ardness, Mama? Is that who your friend is now?"

"Yes. Jeannie made a brilliant marriage," Mrs. Grenville answered. "But the Duke was much older than she was, and I thought when I met him that he was rather a frightening man."

"While you fell in love with Papa."

Mrs. Grenville's eyes lit up.

"I loved him the moment I saw him," she answered. "It was not only that he was so handsome and so very attractive in his uniform. There was something else—something so magical and indescribable that it is difficult to put it into words."

"It was love at first sight!" Leona said with a smile. "And Papa often told me how he fell in love with you."

"Tell me what he said," Mrs. Grenville asked eagerly.

"He walked into the Ball-Room feeling rather bored," Leona related. "He said he had been to so many dances and found the Scottish women dull, with nothing original to say, and he was wishing he was back in the south."

"Go on!" Mrs. Grenville prompted, and for a moment her face was as happy as a young girl's.

"Then Papa saw you!" Leona continued. "You

were dancing very gaily with an officer in the Black Watch whom he knew. He looked at you and he said to himself: 'That is the girl I am going to marry!' "

"And as soon as he spoke to me, I wanted to marry him," Mrs. Grenville cried. "It was just as if we had known each other before and found each other again after a long separation."

"I am sure that is what happens when one is really in love," Leona said almost as if she spoke to herself.

"You will feel like that one day, my darling," Mrs. Grenville said, "then you will understand that when it happens nothing else in the world is of any consequence."

Her voice throbbed as she went on:

"I would have gone with your father anywhere he wished to take me. I would have followed him barefoot to England if he had tried to leave me behind!"

"So you were not envious of your friend marrying a Duke?" Leona teased.

"I have been envious of no-one," Mrs. Grenville answered. "I was so lucky, so unbelievably and marvellously lucky to marry your father!"

"Papa felt just the same."

"He is near me," Mrs. Grenville said almost fiercely. "He has not left me. I cannot see him, but I know he is there!"

"I am sure he is, Mama."

"And that is why I must go to him as soon as I can—you do understand, darling?"

"I will try, Mama."

"Post the letter! Post the letter quickly!" Mrs. Grenville urged. "Then neither your father nor I will have to worry about you."

The letter had been despatched, but before there was any chance of an answer Mrs. Grenville slipped away to join the husband she had loved so deeply.

Leona had found her dead in her bed one morning with a smile on her lips and looking incredibly young.

She had been buried beside her husband in the Church-yard of the little grey Church, and after the funeral was over Leona had gone back to the Manor House to wonder what she should do.

The answer came a week later when she received a letter not from the Duchess but from the Duke of Ardness, and it was addressed to her mother.

It told Mrs. Grenville briefly that her friend the Duchess was dead, but went on:

Nevertheless, if as you say you have not long to live, then I shall be delighted to welcome your daugher here in Scotland.

Tell her that, when the unhappy moment comes and she finds herself alone, she may write to me for further instructions. In the meantime, I hope your fears are groundless and that you will recover your good health.

It was a pleasant letter and because there was nothing else she could do, Leona sat down and replied to it immediately.

She told the Duke that her mother was dead and, while she had no wish to be a burden upon him, she would be very grateful if she could come to Scotland and at least discuss with him her future.

Because she felt quite certain he would acquiesce to her request, she looked round for a purchaser for the house, and disposed of the live-stock on the farm and even the two horses which she loved.

She took the greatest care to find them a home where they would be well looked after.

Fortunately, the neighbouring farmer was, as Leona knew, a kindly man.

He bought the horses and gave her, she thought, more than he would have bid in a sale, simply because he was sorry for her.

He also promised to try to find a purchaser for the house and land.

This, Leona realised, was not going to be easy, but even a small sum would give her a little financial security.

From the money obtained by the sale of the horses there was little left after she had paid all the outstanding bills and given the man who had groomed the horses enough to live on until he found another job.

It was only when everything had been arranged that Leona wondered rather nervously what would happen if the Duke after all refused to have her.

But her fears were groundless.

She received a letter telling her how welcome she would be at Ardness Castle and instructing her to leave immediately.

She was to take the train to Edinburgh, where the Duke's carriage would be waiting for her to complete the last part of the journey.

"Bring an Abigail to look after you," the Duke had written, "and I enclose a Note of Hand for the purchase of two First Class tickets."

This final instruction left Leona in a quandary.

They had employed no live-in servants since her father's death and had made do with women who came from the village to clean the house and charged very little for it.

She was quite certain that if she asked any of the local women to travel with her to Scotland they would be horrified at the idea.

Especially as they would be expected to do so in one of the noisy, smoking trains which were regarded fearfully by the inhabitants of Essex, as if they were prehistoric monsters!

"I must go alone," Leona told herself, "and explain to the Duke when I get there that there was not a houseful of servants from whom to choose a companion."

She thought it unlikely that he would understand how poor they were or in what very different circumstances her mother had lived from her friend the Duchess.

Thinking about it, she realised for the first time that the Duke might think she looked a pauper in her plain gowns which she had made herself with her mother's help.

She had no idea in what sort of state the Duke lived, but she had heard her mother talk of the great Castles inhabited by the Chiefs of the various Clans and of the noble Mansions in Edinburgh where she had attended Balls as a girl.

Leona looked about her at the crumbling and thread-bare appearance of her own home.

There had never been enough money for repairs or alterations, and only now when she was leaving it did she realise that its attraction lay in the people who had lived there, not in the house itself.

'The Duke must take me as I am,' she thought with practical good sense.

But even before she boarded the train she realised that her gowns had not the fullness nor the swing of the crinolines worn by other lady travellers, that her bonnet was trimmed only with cheap ribbons, and her luggage looked more suited to a passenger in the Third Class than in the First.

She had no idea, however, that many of the gentlemen on the platform looked at her and looked again.

It was not her clothes they noticed, but her small oval face with its large, worried grey eyes, and her fair hair, soft as a young child's which framed the clear transparency of her skin.

Leona had a tiny straight nose and sweetly curved lips which smiled trustingly at life; for except for the loss of her parents she had never known unhappiness.

A porter found her a compartment for "Ladies Only" and she travelled in what seemed to her to be extraordinary comfort towards Edinburgh.

She found, as the journey took a long time, that she had not brought enough food with her, but fortu-

nately she was able to restock her wicker basket at
the main stations at which they stopped.

When finally they reached Edinburgh she did not
feel tired or exhausted, but merely excited at what lay
ahead.

The Duke's carriage looked more luxurious than
any vehicle she had ever seen before, with soft pad-
ded cushions and a fur rug which at first she thought
would be unnecessary for the warm days of late
August.

And the silver accoutrements were breath-tak-
ing!

So also were the four horses which drew it and
the out-riders in their dark green livery and polished,
crested silver buttons.

Leona thought the servants seemed surprised
that she was alone, but they looked after her with care
and consideration. When they stayed the night at a
Posting-Inn, every possible arrangement was made
for her comfort.

Ardness was a small County on the east coast of
Scotland between Inverness and Ross.

Leona had looked it up on the map and saw that
travelling from Edinburgh they would have to move
some way north before they crossed the boundary into
Ardness.

She knew on the second day, when they set off
early in the morning, that the roads were rougher
than they had been previously and the country was
certainly wilder.

Now there were few hamlets and they would
drive for perhaps an hour without seeing anyone on
the purple moors or encountering a traveller on the
road.

But it was so lovely that to Leona it was a dream
come true.

'No wonder Mama missed Scotland!' she thought
to herself, and knew it was even more beautiful than
she had imagined.

It was only after they had stopped for a delicious
picnic luncheon, for which Leona had found that far

too much food was provided, that the weather changed.

There had been a slight wind during the morning, but now it began to blow roughly and penetratingly from the sea, and there were scuds of torrential rain which made her feel sorry for the horses.

They had been climbing for the best part of an hour and now they were driving on a narrow road over a treeless and barren moor.

The wind was so chill that Leona was thankful for the fur rug and wished in fact that she had taken from her trunk a warm shawl to put round her shoulders.

She pulled the rug a little closer round her and hoped that the wind and rain would not delay them until it was dark.

She had a feeling it would be very eerie to be on the moors when darkness fell and she was sure that the lanterns on the carriage would given an inadequate light by which to find their way.

The wind seemed to be increasing.

She thought that the two coachmen sitting on the box must by this time be wet through and in danger of losing their tall hats with every violent gust which shook the carriage almost as if it were a rat in the mouth of a terrier.

After the sunshine and warmth of the day before, it seemed extraordinary to Leona that the elements could have changed so completely.

Then, as they reached what seemed to be the very top of a steep incline, there was a sudden grinding sound.

The carriage stopped with a shivering jerk and she gave a cry of fear.

* * *

Leona came slowly back to consciousness to the sound of voices.

Someone was giving instructions while she could hear the horses plunging about and the coachmen talking to them soothingly.

She realised that she was no longer in the carriage but lying on the ground, and she opened her eyes to see a man's face not far from hers.

She looked at him hazily, thinking she had never seen him before and that he was exceedingly good-looking.

Then he said quietly:

"You are all right. Do not be frightened!"

"I . . . I am . . . not," she tried to say, but was conscious that her forehead hurt and it was difficult to speak.

"I think I had better get the lady to the Castle," she heard the man who she now realised was kneeling beside her say. "I will send my men to help you right the carriage and take the horses to my stables."

"Verry gude, M'Lord."

The man who had spoken was undoing the Cairngorm brooch on his left shoulder, which held his plaid.

"Do you think you can sit up?" he asked Leona. "If you can, I will wrap my plaid round you and it will keep you warm. The quickest way to get you out of the wind and rain is on my horse."

He put his arm round Leona as he spoke and helped her to sit up.

He covered her head and shoulders with his plaid, then taking her up in his arms walked a few paces to where, she saw, a horse was standing, held by a groom.

Very gently he lifted her onto the saddle, giving instructions as he did so to one of the dismounted outriders to hold her steady. Then lithely he sprang up behind her and put his arm round her.

Because she was still feeling bemused and dazed from the blow on her head, Leona found it difficult to realise what had happened, until as they started to move she looked back.

She saw the Duke's carriage lying drunkenly against the verge of the road and the horses already free of their shafts.

Then the violence of the wind made her turn her

face towards the man who held her and she laid her cheek against his shoulder.

She felt his arm tighten and he said:

"It is not far to my Castle, but it would have taken far too long to fetch a carriage to convey you there."

"I . . . I am very . . . grateful," Leona managed to say.

"It was fortunate that I saw the accident."

They rode on for some way with the wind blowing the cold even through the thickness of the plaid, so that Leona was grateful for the warmth of her rescuer's body.

Instinctively she moved a little nearer to him. Then as she glanced up she saw there was a smile on his lips above a very firm chin.

"Are you all right?" he asked.

"I think I must have . . . hurt my head . . . against the side of the . . . window," Leona answered. "But . . . there is no . . . other damage."

"We will make sure of that when I get you safely home," he replied.

Even as he spoke the wind seemed to sweep away the words from his lips and Leona thought it wiser not to talk.

They were descending a hill and he held her firmly to prevent her from slipping forward.

There was something comforting, she thought, in the strength of his arm. She felt safe and protected, something she had not known since her father had died.

"This is an adventure!" she told herself, and she wished she could tell her mother what had happened.

She wondered who her rescuer was.

He had been addressed as "M'Lord," so she was aware he was someone of importance, even though she told herself she would have known it anyway.

There was something authoritative in the way he had spoken and the manner in which he had taken command of the situation.

'How lucky he was there!' she thought.

It would have been exceedingly uncomfortable if she had been forced to spend the night on the moors with the wind blowing colder every moment.

They must have reached the bottom of the incline and now the horse was moving quicker and they seemed to be out of the wind.

Leona raised her face a little so that she could see, and she realised they had passed through a pair of wrought-iron gates with a lodge on either side of them.

"We are home," said the man who held her. "You will be able to rest and we can find out if there are any bones broken."

"I promise you . . . it is not as . . . bad as that!" Leona replied.

"I hope not!" he answered.

The horse came to a standstill, and Leona, lifting her head from his shoulder, saw that they were outside a heavy oak door.

She looked up and saw the walls of a Castle rising above her, but there was little time for observation because servants came hurrying through the open door and one of them lifted her gently from the saddle.

She had, although it seemed absurd, almost a feeling of regret because she must leave the comfort and protection of the arms which had held her.

But before she had time to think he had taken her from the servant and was carrying her into the Castle.

"P-please . . . I am sure I can . . . walk," Leona protested.

"There is no need," he answered. "I cannot believe you wish to negotiate a flight of stairs at this moment."

He started to climb them as he spoke and Leona saw that the walls were covered with pictures, shields, pikes, claymores, and flags.

'It is exactly,' she thought with delight, 'as Mama described what the inside of a Castle was like!'

Her rescuer carried her apparently without any exertion on his part to the top of the staircase and as a servant came running up behind him he said:

"I will take the lady to the Thistle Chamber."

"Aye, M'Lord."

The servant moved ahead.

Leona had a quick glimpse of a Salon, and of the walls of the corridor, also hung with shields and pikes. Then she was carried into a large bed-room and set down on a bed.

"Fetch Mrs. McCray!"

"Aye, M'Lord."

The servant vanished and Leona pushed back the plaid.

"Thank you . . . very much," she said automatically, and for the first time she was able to look at her rescuer.

He was, she thought at first glance, exceedingly handsome, and she saw that he was wearing a kilt in a tartan she did not recognise.

It was a pleasing mixture of blues with a red line which echoed in the plaid with which he had covered her. A silver and leather sporran hung from his waist.

He drew his bonnet from his dark head and stood looking at her with a smile on his firm lips.

"You do not look very much the worse for your accident, but we must take no chances."

"I assure you that I am very little harmed," Leona replied, "and I am exceedingly grateful for your kindness in bringing me here."

"The pleasure is mine. May I introduce myself? I am Strathcairn."

Leona gave a little cry.

"I have heard of you," she said, "or at least of your Clan, the McCairns."

"I am gratified," Lord Strathcairn replied. "Will you tell me your name?"

"Leona Grenville."

"Then welcome to Cairn Castle, Miss Grenville. I have gathered that you are a guest of the Duke of Ardness."

"I am," Leona answered, "and I hope His Grace will not be annoyed that I shall be so late in arriving."

"It would be impossible for you to reach his Castle tonight," Lord Strathcairn replied, "even if I thought it wise to send you there in one of my own carriages."

Leona looked worried and he went on:

"But I will despatch a groom to inform His Grace of what has occurred. I feel that whatever damage there has been to your carriage can be repaired by the morning, when you can proceed on your journey."

"Thank you," Leona said. "That is very kind. At the same time, I hope it is not causing you a great deal of trouble to let me stay here."

"I think you know the answer to that," Lord Strathcairn said with a smile. "And what I suggest is that you rest for an hour or so and then, if you feel well enough, perhaps you will give me the pleasure of dining with me."

As he spoke there came a knock on the door.

It opened to reveal an elderly woman.

She was dressed in black and wore a large bunch of keys which hung from her waist.

She curtseyed.

"Ye sent for me, M'Lord?"

"Yes, Mrs. McCray. We have a guest who has had an unfortunate accident. I feel sure I can leave her in your capable hands."

"Indeed ye can, M'Lord."

Lord Strathcairn walked towards the door.

"I shall be very disappointed, Miss Grenville," he said as he reached it, "if you do not feel well enough to dine with me this evening."

Mrs. McCray bustled towards the bed.

"What happened to ye, Miss? Are ye hurt?"

"No, indeed. The carriage turned over," Leona replied, "and I must have hit my head against the window. It knocked me unconscious for a few minutes, but that was all."

"It's quite enough!" Mrs. McCray said. "The road can be awfu' treacherous at any time o' the year.

And as I've said many a time, in the winter it's a death-trap."

Talking away about the iniquities of the road and the difficulties of travel, Mrs. McCray applied her own remedies to the bruise on Leona's forehead.

She then fetched her a warm drink containing honey and what Leona suspected was a spoonful of whisky. After that she took off her clothes and settled down for a proper rest.

It was certainly the warm drink which made her sleep and she awoke to find the maids bringing in hot water for a bath and unpacking her trunk, which had been brought to the Castle from the overturned coach.

She could still hear the wind whistling outside the windows, but a fire had been lit in her room and there was something very luxurious about bathing in front of it in brown water.

Her mother had often described to her how soft and delightful the peat made the water in Scotland, and how good it was for the skin.

As she washed herself Leona knew her mother had not exaggerated.

She had a small choice of gowns in which to dine with Lord Strathcairn and she chose one she had made herself. It was pale pink and had a bertha of old lace which had embellished quite a number of her mother's gowns over the years.

It was not as full as she would have liked, but the tight bodice revealed the gentle curves of her figure and the slimness of her waist.

When she had arranged her hair she hoped that His Lordship would not think her too dowdy a guest.

"Ye look very nice, Miss, if I may say so," Mrs. McCray said encouragingly as she led Leona down the wide corridor along which Lord Strathcairn had carried her.

Now she could admire the shields and pikes on the walls and when they reached the doorway into the Salon she saw that it was a very fine room.

On the first floor, it was large, as were all the

main rooms in Scottish Castles, but at the same time there was a comfort about it which made it not in the least awe-inspiring.

There were book-cases covering one wall, a number of pictures, and a large stone fireplace. The mullioned windows which reached almost to the ceiling had comfortable window-seats covered with velvet cushions in front of them.

Lord Strathcairn was waiting on the hearth and as he came forward to greet her Leona thought she had never seen a man look so impressive.

His kilt in the McCairn tartan was very becoming, and his sporran was far more elaborate than the one he had worn earlier in the day. His jacket was embellished with silver buttons and there was a froth of lace at his throat.

He wore the tartan hose of his Clan and as he moved Leona had a glimpse of the topaz-topped skean-dhu on his left leg.

"You are better, Miss Grenville?" Lord Strathcairn asked.

"I am quite well, thanks to Your Lordship's kindness," Leona replied.

"I am very relieved to hear that."

"I am so impressed by your Castle, My Lord. May I please look out the window?"

She did not wait for his permission but walked towards the window, then gave a cry of delight.

Her bed-room overlooked the garden, but from the windows of the Salon she saw stretched in front of her a large Loch.

There were hills all round it except in the far distance where they divided and she guessed even before Lord Strathcairn told her that from there the river ran down to the sea.

The sun had sunk, but there was still a glow in the sky and the water of the Loch was touched with gold.

The hills surrounding it were blue in the shadows and there were strange lights on them, giving them an almost indescribable beauty.

"It is lovely! The loveliest place I have ever seen!" Leona said with a note of awe in her voice.

"It makes me very happy to hear you say that," Lord Strathcairn replied.

"This Castle must be very old?"

"Parts of it were built over seven hundred years ago," he answered.

"Then there is a great history behind it."

"I shall be only too glad to tell you some of it," Lord Strathcairn answered, "but I must not bore you and I am interested to know why you are in Scotland."

He handed her a glass of sherry and Leona said:

"My parents are dead, but shortly before my mother died she wrote to the Duchess of Ardness, asking her to look after me."

"The Duchess?" Lord Strathcairn queried. "But she also is dead."

"Yes, I know that now," Leona replied. "The Duke told me so in his letter, but he has invited me just the same to make my home with him."

She was aware that Lord Strathcairn stiffened. Then he said in a strange tone she had not heard him use before:

"To make your home with him? I thought perhaps you were just a guest coming north for a short visit."

"No, indeed," Leona replied. "I have nowhere else to go, but I would not wish to be an encumbrance upon His Grace, and perhaps if he tires of having me at the Castle I could find employment of some sort in Edinburgh."

"I think that extremely unlikely," Lord Strathcairn said sharply. "At the same time, I do not like . . ."

He stopped, but Leona felt that it was with an effort.

She looked at him enquiringly and as she did so the Butler announced:

"Dinner is served, M'Lord!"

The Dining-Room, which was on the same floor,

was almost as impressive as the Salon. The table was loaded with silver ornaments and large goblets which Leona was sure were of great antiquity.

The room itself seemed mediaeval with a heavily carved stone fireplace and high narrow windows stretching to the beamed ceiling.

They were covered with dark red velvet curtains, and with two candelabra lighted on the table the room seemed warm and, despite its size, cosy.

Leona looked at the candelabra and gave a faint smile.

"What is amusing you, Miss Grenville?" Lord Strathcairn asked, and she wondered that he was so perceptive as to notice.

"When I looked at your candelabra," she answered, "I was thinking of a story my mother told me about one of her ancestors."

"I think I know the one to which you are referring," Lord Strathcairn said, "but tell me all the same."

"He was Macdonald of Keppoch, and one of his guests tried to impress him with stories of the great candelabras to be seen in the houses of England."

Lord Strathcairn smiled.

"Of course I remember the tale! He ringed his table with tall Clansmen each holding aloft a flaming pine-knot!"

"That is right!" Leona exclaimed. "Then he grinned at his guest and asked where in England, France, or Italy was there a house with such candle-sticks!"

"I am sorry that I cannot offer you anything so sensational," Lord Strathcairn said.

"Everything I see is a delight in itself," Leona answered. "I cannot tell you how much it means to me to be in Scotland!"

"So your mother was a Macdonald? I think it would be easy to find that we are related. There are quite a number of Macdonalds in my family-tree."

"Papa used to say that the Scots turned up everywhere! There was no stopping them!" Leona said with a mischievous smile.

"I am delighted to welcome you as a kins-woman."

As the meal progressed Leona thought she had never enjoyed a dinner more.

There was salmon from the Loch, which Lord Strathcairn said he had caught that morning, and grouse from the moors, which he had shot the previous day.

It was the first time she had ever dined alone with a man and Lord Strathcairn explained to her that he lived alone except when occasionally one of his relatives came to stay with him.

"One of my Aunts was here recently," he said, "and only last week returned to Edinburgh."

He glanced round at the large array of servants who were waiting on them and added:

"I hope you will feel that you are adequately chaperoned. Mrs. McCray has arranged for one of the maids to sleep in the dressing-room of your bed-chamber."

"I feel I am quite safe with you," Leona answered.

It was true, she thought, that ever since he had put her on his horse and put his arm round her, she had felt safe and somehow protected by his very presence.

She realised that her answer pleased him.

"Do you really feel that," he asked, "or are you just being polite?"

"I am speaking the . . . truth," Leona said in a low voice.

Her eyes met his and somehow something strange passed between them, something she could not explain to herself.

After a moment Lord Strathcairn said:

"I want to be sure of that. Will you remember that, wherever else you may be in Scotland, there is always a place for you here in the Castle, and I am always at your service."

"Thank . . . you," Leona answered.

She wondered why it was difficult to speak.

Again her eyes were held by his. Then, as it seemed as if he was about to say something else, there came the high notes of the pipes, which grew louder as the piper entered the Dining-Room.

Wearing the full dress of the McCairn Clan, he strode round and round the table, his kilt swinging and his music calling up the memories of Highland wars and Highland dreams.

Leona remembered her mother telling her that the greatest of all pipers in the Highlands were the MacCrimmonses, who could make men weep or fight like gods just by playing on their flutes of bone.

Every Chieftain, she knew, had his piper who awoke him in the morning and played to him during the last meal of the day.

When a Chieftain went to war, his piper marched behind him with the wild music of the pipes spurring men on to new deeds of valour as he played of those that were past.

The piper played three tunes, then stopped beside Lord Strathcairn to salute him and accept from his hand a small silver cup filled with whisky.

He raised it in a toast, poured it down his throat, saluted again, and left the Dining-Room.

"That is something I have longed to hear," Leona said.

"The pipes?" Lord Strathcairn asked.

"I know now, having heard them, that I am indeed a Scot!"

"The music draws you?"

"It makes me feel wild and excited, and it makes me proud and a little sad. It makes me realise too that the Scottish spirit is unconquerable."

She spoke with a sincerity which seemed to come from her very heart.

Lord Strathcairn reached out and took her hand in his.

"Thank you," he said quietly.

Then as he kissed her fingers she felt a very different emotion, but which in its way was even more wonderful!

Chapter Two

Lord Strathcairn rose from his high-backed chair and asked:

"Would you like to see some Highland dancing?"

"I would love it!" Leona replied. "But should I not leave you to your port?"

"I think I have no need of port this evening," he replied, and led her from the Dining-Hall and up the stone stairs to the floor above.

Leona's mother had told her that in all Scottish Castles there was what was known as the "Chief's Room," which was where the Chief of a Clan received his followers, where plans of battle were discussed, and where he entertained.

Leona had imagined a large and impressive Baronial Hall, but the one they entered took her completely by surprise.

It must have run the whole length of the Castle. There was a Musicians' Gallery at one end and the walls were decorated with stags' heads and antlers, and with shields and claymores.

But the most unusual feature about it was the ceiling covered in wood and bearing the Strathcairn Arms.

There was, as might have been expected, a large open fireplace in which huge logs were burning and round the room waiting were a number of Clansmen all wearing the Strathcairn tartan.

They were very colourful, but Leona knew that

23

the tartans were of comparatively modern origin; in the past, it was not a Highlander's kilt—which was little more than a piece of cloth—which denoted his Clan, but his slogan and his badge.

Every tribe had its slogan, a wild savage exhortation to slaughter or to reminder of the heroic past, and every Clan's identity was determined by its badge of heather, oak, myrtle, or gule, which a man wore in his bonnet.

Each plant had its mystic significance and was a charm against witchcraft and disaster, or else it had its origin in the necessities of the Clan's life, like the badge of the MacNeils, which was sea-weed.

"It is with sea-weed," Mrs. Grenville had explained, "that the MacNeils manure the barren fields of their western islands."

But in the well-cut kilts with their swinging pleats worn by the McCairns there was little to remind the on-looker of the parti-coloured faded cloth which the Highlanders had called a "braecan."

Lord Strathcairn led Leona to a small platform near the Musicians' Gallery on which were arranged two high-backed chairs carved with heraldic designs.

They seated themselves and immediately the Clansmen began to dance.

Leona had always been told of the lightness and agility that the men of Scotland showed in their dancing, and now she could see for herself that the stories were not exaggerated.

They danced with pointed toes over crossed swords, they danced reels, and as the bagpipes swirled and wailed, Leona thought it was more fascinating than anything she had ever seen before.

She thought too that Lord Strathcairn looked every inch a Chieftain as he sat beside her and she remembered how in the past the Chieftains in Scotland had been the Kings of their Glen.

"A Chief protected his Clan, and they would follow him and obey him whatever he might ask of them," her mother had said.

But then, Mrs. Grenville had added sadly:

"Alas, the Highlanders have been forgotten by their Chiefs, and without them they are lost!"

They did not understand life without a leader.

Leona learnt that even in the Sixteenth and Seventeenth Centuries the Chief of a Scottish Clan was a man whose understanding and experience was often far wider than that of most Englishmen.

"A Chieftain could speak English and Gaelic," Mrs. Grenville had said, "and very often Greek, French, and Latin as well. He sent his sons to be educated at Universities in Glasgow, Edinburgh, Paris, and Rome!"

She smiled as she continued:

"He drank French claret, wore lace at his throat, and his pastimes were based on the land and the culture of his people."

Again she had looked sad as she added:

"But now the Chiefs are no longer content with shooting the stag, the wolf, the wild cat, and the grouse. They have gone south, leaving their people like ships without rudders."

Watching Lord Strathcairn taking an interest in the dancing, Leona thought that here was a Chief who was concerned with his people.

She wished that her mother could be with her, for she knew that she would have been as thrilled as she was by the dancing and the whole picture which the Chief's Room presented.

When the Clansmen had finished, Lord Strathcairn introduced many of his men to Leona.

She noticed that while he told his men that she had Macdonald blood in her veins and this was her first visit to the Highlands, he did not mention that she was to be the guest of the Duke of Ardness.

She had a feeling that there was some constraint between the Duke and her host and she tried to remember if she had ever heard of any feud between the McCairns and the MacArdns.

She wished now that she could remember more

of what her mother had told her when she had talked so often of Scotland and related the colourful legends of the campaigns and the superstitions that were so much a part of her blood.

Far away in the south of England, it had seemed unreal.

But now that she was actually in Scotland, Leona felt herself responding to everything round her, just as she had felt the first notes of the pipes bring her a strange excitement and exaltation she had never known before.

Finally, having congratulated the dancers, Lord Strathcairn escorted Leona back to the Salon on the first floor.

"Thank you," she said. "Thank you more than I can say."

"You enjoyed it?" he asked.

"It was very exciting," she answered, "and Mama was right when she said that no-one could be so light on his feet as a Scotsman dancing a reel!"

Lord Strathcairn went to the grog-tray which stood in one corner of the Salon and poured Leona a glass of lemonade.

When he had done so they moved towards the hearth and stood in front of the log-fire, the flames picking out the gold in Leona's hair so that she seemed almost to have a halo of light round her head.

As they stood there they heard the wind whistling round the Castle and the rain beating on the windows.

"I am blessing that wind for having blown you here tonight," Lord Strathcairn said in his deep voice. "It is something I never expected."

"For me it has been an enchantment," Leona said.

As she spoke she raised her eyes to his and once again was held strangely spellbound by the expression in his.

"You are very beautiful!" he said.

There was a note in his voice which brought the colour to her cheeks.

Because she was shy she looked away from him into the flames.

There was silence. Then, thinking again how he looked exactly as a Chieftain should, she asked:

"Do you stay here all the year round?"

"This is my home, my life," he said. "This is where I live!"

To her surprise, he spoke in what suddenly seemed a very different tone of voice.

There was something sharp, almost hard, in the way he answered her, and as she looked at him in surprise he said:

"I am sure you are tired, Miss Grenville. It has been an exhausting day for you. You will therefore wish to retire."

His manner made Leona feel that he had withdrawn from her and he was no longer close and protective as he had seemed ever since taking care of her after the accident.

She longed to say she had no wish to go to bed, but wanted to stay talking to him.

There was so much she wanted to learn, so much she wanted to hear. But she thought that it would seem forward to suggest such a thing. Perhaps in fact he was already bored with her company.

She suddenly felt very young and inexperienced.

Perhaps, she told herself humbly, she should have suggested going to bed the moment they had left the Chief's Room.

Instead, she had allowed him to show that he was ready to be rid of her and therefore put her in a humiliating position.

"May I thank you for being so very kind?" she asked.

Her eyes sought his pleadingly, but he was looking away from her. In fact he led the way across the room, opening the door and stepping out into the corridor.

"You will find Mrs. McCray waiting for you," he said. "Good-night, Miss Grenville."

"Good-night, My Lord."

Leona curtseyed, and as she walked away down the corridor, alone, she was aware that he had gone back into the Salon.

"What did I say? Why did he change?" she asked herself when she was in bed and the light from the fire cast strange shadows round the room.

She could hear again the softness of his voice as had said: "You are very beautiful!"

Then suddenly after her simple question there had been a sharpness in his tone that was undeniable, and she had felt almost as if he had thrust her to one side.

"I cannot understand it," Leona told herself unhappily, and she was still worrying about it when she fell asleep.

* * *

"It's a fine morning, Miss, and the wind's gone," Mrs. McCray announced.

She pulled back the curtains, and as she did so Leona could hear the music of the pipes on the other side of the house.

The sun came in through the windows, casting a golden glow. The worries of the night seemed to have disappeared and she wanted to be up and perhaps to breakfast with Lord Strathcairn.

But Mrs. McCray had other ideas.

"I've brought your breakfast up, Miss, seeing you might be tired after your experience of yesterday."

"I feel in perfect health this morning!" Leona replied.

She glanced at the heavy tray the housemaid was bringing into the room to set down by her bed, and ventured somewhat tentatively:

"Will not his . . . Lordship expect me to . . . breakfast with him?"

"His Lordship had breakfast an hour since," Mrs. McCray replied. "He's an early riser, but he suggests that when ye are dressed, Miss, ye might like to see the gardens afore ye depart."

"Yes, of course, I should like that very much!" Leona agreed.

She ate quickly and afterwards, as she dressed Mrs. McCray assisted her and a housemaid packed her trunk.

Leona had half hoped it would either be such a rough and windy day that she could not proceed on her journey, or that the Duke's carriage would not be repaired in time to take her.

As she said good-bye to Mrs. McCray and left her room, she found that two footmen were outside waiting to carry her trunk down to the carriage, which she gathered was already at the front door.

She had an uneasy feeling that she was being hurried into doing something she did not wish to do, and she admitted to herself that she wanted to stay on at Cairn Castle rather than proceed to Ardness.

'It is ridiculous of me,' she thought as she reached the Salon, 'but I feel as if I am leaving something very precious.'

Her introspective thoughts, however, were forgotten when she saw Lord Strathcairn, who was sitting at his writing-desk.

He rose as she entered and Leona found she had to repress an impulse to run towards him and tell him how glad she was to see him.

Instead, she curtseyed formally as he said gravely:

"Good-morning, Miss Grenville."

"Good-morning, My Lord."

"You slept well "

"Very well, thank you."

"As you can see," he said, "the wind has died away in the night and it is now a day of sunshine and warmth."

"Mrs. McCray said that you would show me the gardens."

"If that would please you."

"I would love to see them!"

"I think you will find them rather beautiful," he

said. "They were laid out by my mother and I have always tried to carry out her wishes."

They descended the stairs and when they reached the gardens by a side door of the Castle, Leona could understand that Lord Strathcairn was justifiably proud of them.

Sloping down from the Castle to the very edge of the Loch, they were protected on either side by shrubs and there were many plants and flowers that one would not expect to find in the Highlands.

And yet today the sun was very warm and the hills on either side of the Loch seemed protective.

Now as Leona looked over the expanse of silver water she could see that there were many little crofts on either side of it nestling in the shadow of the hills, and in the green holdings she saw the shaggy Highland cattle with their huge horns.

"Do you own a great deal of land?" Leona asked.

"Not as much as I should like," Lord Strathcairn replied, "but I have many acres stretching eastwards to the sea and south into Inverness-shire."

"And north?" Leona asked.

It seemed to her that the expression in his eyes darkened.

"My boundary is at the top of the moor. After that, one is in Ardness."

"As near as that?" Leona exclaimed. "Then how far is the Castle?"

"By road," Lord Strathcairn replied, "you will have to travel nearly ten miles before you reach your destination, but as the crow flies we are not more than perhaps three miles from it."

"How extraordinary!" Leona exclaimed.

"There are many gorges, crevasses, and burns to cross," he explained, "and when the latter are in spate they can easily sweep away a road unless it is built high above them."

"I can understand that," Leona said.

They had been walking down towards the Loch as they talked and now she turned round to look at the Castle behind her.

She gave a little cry of delight.

"But it is lovely!" she exclaimed. "It is like a fairy Castle. I had no idea it could be so beautiful!"

It was in fact very romantic. Built of grey stone, the walls rose high to be surmounted near the top with corbelled turrets.

Like the dancers she had seen last night, Leona thought, it had a lightness about it that one would not have expected in such a large building.

"I can understand why it means so much to you," she said to Lord Strathcairn.

"As I said last night," he replied, "it is my home and this is where I must live if I am to look after my people and protect my Clan."

Leona was just about to say how glad she was that he felt like that when he changed the subject.

"I think, Miss Grenville," he said, "that as His Grace will be expecting you and the carriage is at the door, you should start your journey."

"Yes . . . of course," Leona agreed.

Again she felt flustered, because she thought she herself should have suggested leaving and not have waited for her host to point out to her her duty.

At the same time, she had a reluctance to go from the sunshine of the garden.

Deliberately she turned to look again at the Loch.

"I hope, now that I am in Scotland, I shall have a chance to see someone catch a salmon," she said. "My father, who loved fishing, often told me how exciting it is!"

"One is often disappointed," Lord Strathcairn replied, "just as in life one is disappointed in many things."

He seemed to Leona to be already moving towards the Castle, and because she could think of no more ways in which to delay her departure she followed him somewhat forlornly.

She looked up at the distant moor.

"How do you know when you reach your boundary?" she asked. "Is there anything to indicate it?"

"I think my gillies know every inch of the ground so well that they can tell me which piece of heather is in Ardness and which is mine," Lord Strathcairn remarked. "But on top of the moor is a large cairn which must have been there for centuries—and that is how I know when I have reached my boundary."

They were nearing the Castle and now as they came up the path from the gardens Leona could see the horses waiting outside the front door.

"It was . . . so kind of you to . . . have me here last night," she said. "I hope we shall . . . meet again soon."

"I think that unlikely."

Leona stopped walking to look at Lord Strathcairn, her eyes very wide in surprise.

"B-but . . . why?" she asked.

"His Grace and I do not agree on certain subjects," Lord Strathcairn replied.

"I . . . I was trying to . . . remember if I had heard of any . . . feud between your Clan and the Duke's," Leona said hesitatingly.

"We fought in the past," Lord Strathcairn answered, "but my father and the late Duke declared a truce."

"Which has now been broken?"

"Which has now been broken!"

Lord Strathcairn did not say more, but he took a step forward as if he would convey her quickly to the carriage.

"Then . . . I shall not . . . see you again?" she asked in a low voice.

"I cannot come to Ardness Castle," he replied. "But let me make this quite clear: You are always welcome here and as I told you last night I am at your service."

The warmth was back in his voice and she felt almost as if she was enveloped in sunshine.

"Then . . . if I can . . . call on you . . . ?" she asked hesitatingly.

"I shall be hoping that you will do so."

Lord Strathcairn glanced at the moor behind him.

"It is only a short ride to the cairn," he said, "and then you will be on my property."

"I shall . . . remember that," Leona said a little breathlessly.

His eyes looked down into hers and she thought he was about to say something important. Then even as his lips parted there was an interruption.

A servant came towards them.

"I beg ye pardon, M'Lord, but His Grace's coachmen say that the horses are restless."

"Thank you, Duncan," Lord Strathcairn said. "Miss Grenville is leaving at once."

They walked into the Hall of the Castle to where Leona's travelling-cloak was waiting for her. She put it on and realised that everything else she possessed had been already placed in the carriage.

She held out her hand.

"I thank Your Lordship most sincerely for your hospitality."

He took her hand in his, but he did not kiss it as she had hoped he might. Instead, he bowed, and Leona curtseyed and stepped into the carriage.

As if he was impatient at having been kept waiting, the coachman whipped up the horses and they were off almost before she had time to sit down on the seat.

She bent forward but only had a quick glimpse of Lord Strathcairn standing on the steps, watching her go, before they were proceeding at a sharp pace down the long drive and out onto the moorland road.

When they reached the road on which the coach had been blown over the night before, Leona looked back at the Castle standing on the edge of the Loch.

She put down the window of the carriage so that she could have a good view, and now in the brilliant sunshine she thought again that it was the most beautiful place she had ever seen.

The purple moors, the lights on the water, the

little crofts nestling under the protection of the hills, all seemed even more beautiful than they had before.

And the Castle itself was the perfect embodiment of all the mystery and romance of the Highlands.

"It is wonderful!" Leona told herself with a little sigh, then she could see it no more.

As they drove on she found herself wondering why Lord Strathcairn was in disagreement with the Duke and how it could be so explosive that they could not in fact even meet.

She had not forgotten the expression on his face when she had told him that she was to make her home at Ardness Castle.

Why did it seem to him so strange?

Then she told herself that the Scots had fiery temperaments and never forgave an insult.

She had only to remember the way her mother had spoken of the Campbells to know how deeply they could feel.

'Perhaps I can make them friends, again,' she thought to herself.

She knew she wanted to heal the breach so that she could see Lord Strathcairn again as soon as possible.

The road over which they were journeying was narrow and stony. But the horses were moving at a fair pace and Leona reckoned that they must have covered four or five miles when there was a sudden check and the sound of loud voices.

She looked out the window and saw to her astonishment that a number of people seemed to be congregated round a croft.

There was a lot of shouting, and she saw to her amazement that two men were dragging bedding, tables, a spinning-wheel, and clothing out of the croft while two women and a number of children screamed at them.

People from other crofts were running up the road, so it was impossible for the horses to proceed,

and now Leona saw that the men who had dragged
out the furniture were setting fire to the roof!

It was difficult to take everything in. Then one of
the women holding a baby in her arms screamed out
in Gaelic:

"*Tha mo clann air a bhi air am murt!*" It was followed by a great shout of anger.

"My children are being murdered!"

Leona translated and realised that besides the
two men setting fire to the croft there were three
policeman.

She stepped out of the carriage.

The noise and the shouting was terrifying, but
she could see that the women were trying to save
some hens that were shut up in a coop and were in
danger of being burned alive.

Just as the croft took fire, a man hurried forward
to dive through the flames and emerge carrying a
half-naked and screaming child.

"What is happening What is going on here?"
Leona asked.

It was impossible for her voice to be heard
amongst the general confusion, but a man better
dressed and obviously with more authority than the
rest came forward to say abruptly:

"Ye had best proceed, Ma'am. I'll clear the road
for the horses."

"But what is happening?" Leona asked.

"These people are being evicted, Ma'am."

"Evicted?" Leona exclaimed, then added:

"Do you mean that Clearances are taking place
here?"

"His Grace requires the land, Ma'am."

"For sheep?" Leona asked.

"Aye, that's correct. And now, Ma'am, if ye will
get into the carriage ye'll be able to proceed."

The man to whom she had been speaking turned
away from her as he spoke and Leona realised that
the footman was holding open the carriage door and
was waiting for her to enter it.

"Help—please help!" a woman screamed at her.

She hesitated, wishing to reply, but a policeman struck the woman with a truncheon and she fell to the ground.

Leona wanted to go to her, but as she would have moved towards the woman the man who had spoken to her was again at her side.

"Will ye please leave, Ma'am?" he said sharply. "There is naught ye can do, and His Grace would not wish ye to linger."

Leona wanted to protest about the manner in which the women and children were being treated, but somehow she found herself back in the carriage, the door was shut, and the horses were moving swiftly over the cleared road.

She looked out the window at the burning croft.

Then she realised that the other people who had been watching the first eviction, anticipating what was going to happen, were already taking the furniture from their own houses.

Leona leant back against the carriage seat and felt almost faint at the horror of what she had seen.

She had heard talk of the Evictions and the Highland Clearances ever since she could remember, and the manner in which they had been carried out.

They had made her mother, usually so soft and gentle, rage with anger when she spoke about them, and sometimes weep despairingly.

But it all appeared to have happened long ago in the past, and Leona had not realised until this moment that such cruelty was still being perpetrated.

Her mother had often told her of how in 1762 Sir John Lockhart Ross had introduced sheep-farming in the north and inadvertently destroyed the soul and spirit of the Highlands.

Five hundred of his Cheviot ewes had survived when everyone expected them to die of the harsh climate.

But they had thrived, and as wool was a valuable commodity it had struck the Landlords of the Highlands that here was a new way of making money.

Many Highland Landlords were almost bankrupt and a sudden vision came to them of their hitherto unproductive moors and Glens providing a perfect Sheep-Walk.

But of course the first necessity was to clear the ground of its inhabitants.

For centuries the Highlanders had endured the hard winters, tended their small crofts, and bred their cattle.

They did not believe it when they were told that they must leave the only homes they had ever known and move away from the land which they thought was their own.

They looked to their Chieftains for guidance and received none.

Many of them did not understand that they were required to move down to the sea-shore and scratch a living there, or emigrate to a strange world across the sea.

So their crofts were burned over their heads and they were treated as if they were criminals.

Ever since she had been a child Leona had heard of the sufferings that had been inflicted first in Sutherland, then in Ross.

To her mother it was a betrayal of everything she believed in, everything that was part of her heritage.

But Mrs. Grenville was a long way from home, and it was hard to have a true picture of what had occurred or to understand how there could be no champions of the Highlanders to sponsor their cause.

It had all happened long before Leona was born, and it was only five years ago, in 1845, that the whole controversy and recriminations concerning the Highland Clearances were aroused again by the *Times* newspaper.

The Editor, John Delane, had learnt that ninety Ross-shire cottagers had been removed from Glen-calvie and forced to encamp in the Church-yard as they had no roof over their heads.

The *Times* had hitherto not given much attention to the Highland Clearances, but now John Delane himself had gone to Scotland and arrived in time to witness the departure of the Glencalvie people.

Mrs. Grenville had read aloud his findings as the tears ran lown her cheeks.

Mr. Delane had found that all the cottages in the Glen were empty except for one, where an old pensioner was dying.

The rest of the people were seated on a green brae, the women neatly dressed, wearing scarlet or plain shawls, the men having their shepherd's plaid wrapped about them.

The weather was wet and cold and the people had been marched out of the Glen, with two or three carts filled with their children, to the Church-yard.

John Delane wrote that what was happening in the Highlands was the result of a "cold, calculated heartlessness which was almost as incredible as it was disgusting."

"Why could no-one stop it, Mama?" Leona had asked her mother.

"These people told the Editor of the *Times* that they never saw their Landlord and it was the Factors acting on his behalf who behaved with such brutality."

It had all been very difficult for Leona to understand, but now, hearing the cries of the children and seeing the despair on the faces of those watching their homes being burnt, she felt physically sick with disgust and anger.

And she knew who was responsible.

It was no use blinding herself to the fact that they were travelling over the Duke's land and it was the Duke's tenants who were being thrown out of their crofts.

They would, she knew, have to huddle down by the sea-shore, as in the case of other Clearances those who were evicted were made to do.

The only alternative was to take a ship across the sea, but the emigrants often died of the cold or lack of food on board, or were killed by epidemics of smallpox or typhoid.

'It cannot be true! It cannot be happening all over again!' Leona thought.

She remembered how her mother had cried out against the sheep which had ousted the Highlanders from the Glens and the moors and left behind only the ghosts of those whose courage and endurance had once been the pride of Scotland.

"How can the Duke do this to his own people?" Leona asked.

Now she could understand all too well why Lord Strathcairn had quarrelled with the Duke.

On Lord Strathcairn's land she had seen crofts with their cattle by the side of the Loch.

There had been no flocks of sheep on the ground that he owned, and her heart warmed towards him as she understood now why his people needed him and why, if he would fight for their cause, he must stay amongst them.

Then nervously she wondered what she should say to the Duke or even how she could bite back the words of condemnation which she was afraid would burst from her lips as soon as she met him.

"Perhaps he does not know! Perhaps he does not understand what these people are suffering!" she told herself.

Yet the Evictions were taking place only a few miles from the Castle.

Could he be so blind?

And if he was in residence, unlike so many Landlords of the north who lived in England while their Factors committed such crimes in their name, surely he could not remain in ignorance?

As the horses proceeded over the moorlands, Leona wished she could jump out of the carriage and run back to Cairn Castle.

She wished she were brave enough, and yet it seemed to her that the carriage inexorably carried her on and there was nothing she could do about it.

She felt positively frightened and for the first time she wished she had not come to Scotland but had refused the Duke's offer.

"How can I . . . explain to him what I . . . feel?"
she asked herself.

She remembered the horror in her mother's voice
as she read aloud the reports in the *Times* and related to her how the different Clans had been broken
up and sent to various parts of the world.

She had often quoted Ailean Dall—the blind
Bard of Glengarry—who had written:

A crois has been placed upon us in Scotland,
Poor men are naked beneath it,
Without food, without money, without pasture,
The North is utterly destroyed.

"Ailean Dall chose very significant words," her
mother explained. "'Crois' in Gaelic means more than
'cross.' It is something terrible, close to the sins of
Sodom and Gomorrah."

She gave a deep sigh.

"And the Gaelic word for 'pasture' means not
only meadowland but the idea of peace, happiness,
and tranquillity—something the Highlanders will never
know again."

Even the Macdonalds, Leona learnt, were not
without blame.

Of all the Highland Chiefs, her father had said
once, none disposed of their people more freely than
the Macdonalds of Glengarry and the Chisholms of
Stranglass.

Her mother had not argued, she had merely
wept, and sometimes Leona thought the Clearances
hurt her even more than the thought of the massacre
of Glencoe.

Now she had seen it for herself and she could
understand the horror that had shaken her mother
and made her weep.

"It is wrong! It is wicked!" Leona stormed.

Every mile she drew nearer to Ardness Castle
she felt her anger rising, and yet at the same time she
became more apprehensive.

It seemed to her that she had passed through a

life-time of emotion before finally the carriage began to descend from the high road on which they had travelled ever since they had left Cairn Castle.

It moved down into a deep Glen, the road winding through dark fir-trees beyond which there were heather-covered moors.

There was not a croft in sight, but Leona had glimpses of stone walls without roofs, and she was sure it was not many years since they had been inhabited.

There was a river running through the centre of the Glen.

Presently the road ran beside it, while the mountains rose so sharply on each side and were so high that it made everything seem overshadowed.

And yet it had a majesty and a beauty that was all its own.

It had not the gentle loveliness of the Loch at Cairn Castle, but something more impressive and, to Leona, at the moment more ominous.

She had not realised until she actually reached it that Ardness Castle was so near the sea.

She could see, at the end of the Glen, white-crested waves, and high above the mouth of the river, she saw the Castle.

It was far more impressive, far more awe-inspiring, than she had expected.

It had been built, she was certain, as a defence against both rival Clans and the Vikings, and it was still a giant, impregnable fortress.

With the river running below it and the sea beyond, its grey stone harsh against the surrounding hills, it was most awe-inspiring.

They crossed a bridge over the river and drove through low twisted trees and thick shrubs along a drive.

The great tower nearest to the sea still had its arrowhead slits, but the later addition of grey stone with a trestled roof and Sixteenth Century turrets had long, narrow Gothic windows.

The carriage drew to a standstill. The great door

was a formidable, nail-studded bastion of timber with iron hinges. Stone machicolations were poised high above to deluge an unwelcome visitor with molten lead.

There were a large number of servants, all wearing kilts and seeming to Leona, because she was nervous, to be enormous bearded men, frightening because they were so large.

One who appeared to be in charge led her to a huge square-built Hall and up a wide stone staircase on which their footsteps sounded loud and appeared to echo.

At the top, the servant flung open a door and announced in a stentorian voice:

"Miss Grenville, Ye Grace!"

Leona had the impression of a room far larger than she had expected, with a high arched roof and windows which seemed to let in very little light.

The Duke was standing at the far end in front of a heavily carved fireplace. As she walked towards him she felt as if she had shrunk in size, while he was overpoweringly big.

This was, she found as she reached him, a slight exaggeration arising from her nervousness, but he was in fact tall, grey-bearded, and exceedingly autocratic.

He held himself proudly, but Leona realised that he was an elderly man and his face was deeply lined.

Yet she could understand all too well what her mother had meant when she had said he was intimidating.

The hand he held out to her was so very much larger than her own that she felt as if her fingers were lost in some inescapable trap.

"You have arrived at last!" the Duke exclaimed.

His voice was resonant, and although he was smiling, she had the feeling there was a rebuke behind his words.

Leona curtseyed. Then as she rose she found that the Duke was still holding her hand and looking at her with eyes which were staring at her so penetratingly that it was embarrassing.

"I think you have already learnt, Your Grace, that there was a slight accident yesterday evening."

"Which meant you had to stay at Cairn Castle! That is extremely regrettable. My coachmen should have taken more care of you."

"It was not really their fault," Leona said. "The wind was very fierce and the rain was blinding, so I think the wheels must have run off the road."

"The coachmen will be reprimanded!" the Duke said sharply. "But at least you have arrived!"

"I am here," Leona agreed, "but, Your Grace, I saw a horrible sight on the way."

"What was that?"

She thought the question was something like a pistol-shot.

"An . . . eviction . . . Your Grace."

The Duke did not answer and Leona went on:

"It was the most . . . degrading and the most . . . heart-breaking spectacle I have ever . . . seen."

She meant to speak firmly, but her voice sounded weak and agitated even to herself.

"My mother often spoke of the Clearances," she went on, "but I did not . . . believe they were still taking place . . . not in Ardness!"

"There is only one Glen left, at any rate, in which there are defiant idiots who will not do as they are told," the Duke answered.

"But their crofts were being . . . set on fire!"

"You had no right to stop!" the Duke exclaimed.

"That is not the point," Leona replied. "It was taking place, and . . . one child was nearly . . . burnt alive!"

The Duke made a restless movement and she knew he was angry.

"I think that as you have been travelling for some time you will want to wash before the meal that has been prepared for you," he said coldly. "You will be shown to your bed-chamber."

His hand was on the bell-pull, and although Leona had a great many other things she wished to say, they somehow died on her lips.

She realised that he was brushing her aside as if she were a tiresome insect, and that what she had said had made no impact upon him whatsoever.

Never had she known such a feeling of impotence and helplessness.

Then before she could find her voice again, before she had time to think, she found herself being escorted down a corridor and shown into a large bedroom where a Housekeeper was waiting for her.

There were also two maids, and they all curtseyed.

"I'm Mistress McKenzie," the Housekeeper said. "This is Maggy an' this is Janet. We're all here, Miss, to make ye comfortable."

"Thank you," Leona said.

"And His Grace's instructions are that ye have merely to ask and anything ye require shall be procured for ye."

"Thank you," Leona said again.

She wondered what would happen if she asked for food and clothing to be sent to the families who were being evicted.

It was what she wanted to do, but she knew even as she thought of it that she was not brave enough.

'No wonder Lord Strathcairn has quarrelled with the Duke,' she thought.

She found herself longing to be back in the quiet and safety of Cairn Castle. . . .

Or was it more truly a longing for its . . . owner?

Chapter Three

Leona went towards the wash-stand and one of the maids hurried to pour some hot water into a basin.

"Would ye wish to change, Miss?" Mrs. McKenzie enquired.

"I think I will," Leona replied. "My travelling-gown is thick and today it seems very warm."

"The sun is awfu' hot at midday," Mrs. McKenzie agreed. "Perhaps, Miss, ye'd like to put on one o' your new gowns."

"My new gowns?" Leona exclaimed in surprise.

She realised, having just arrived, that the house-maids had not yet begun unpacking her trunks.

In answer to her question, Mrs. McKenzie crossed the bed-room and opened the door of a wardrobe. Hanging there were half a dozen dresses.

Leona stared at them in astonishment.

"Whose are those?" she enquired.

"They're for ye, Miss," Mrs. McKenzie replied. "His Grace ordered them from Edinburgh an' there are more to come."

"For me?" Leona exclaimed. "B-but why . . . and how did His Grace . . . know my size?"

Mrs. McKenzie smiled.

"His Grace told me, Miss, that he remembered ye mother well an' that she wrote to the Duchess Jean saying ye resembled her closely when she were a girl."

Leona recalled that her mother had said that in the letter which had been despatched to the Duchess.

"Why should His Grace ... wish to give me some ... new gowns?" she questioned. "It is exceedingly kind of him."

"His Grace wishes ye to be happy, Miss, as Ardness Castle is to be your future home."

Leona could not help wondering if it was not rather frightening to think her future was decided for her. Then as if compelled she walked towards the wardrobe.

The gowns were charming; they had the full crinolines she had always longed for and tight bodices to accentuate a tiny waist.

For the evening there were elaborate, beautifully embroidered or embellished berthas and draped skirts ornamented with bunches of artificial flowers.

"They are lovely ... quite lovely!" she exclaimed.

"His Grace hoped ye would think so, Miss," Mrs. McKenzie said with a smile. "He sent the most minute instructions to the best dressmaker in Edinburgh. I'm sure when His Grace sees ye in the gowns he'll not be disappointed."

"I hope not!" Leona said.

She took off her own dress, realising how dowdy and plain it looked by comparison with the new ones.

She chose a pretty day-gown of heavy green silk trimmed with lace round the neck. It buttoned tightly to the waist, then flared out in heavy frills to the ground.

It was so beautiful that she stared at herself in the mirror in astonishment, hardly believing that she could own anything so attractive or feel so well dressed.

"It's just a wee trifle large in the waist, Miss," Mrs. McKenzie was saying, "but now I knows what is wrong I can alter the others. There is a very beautiful gown for ye to wear for dinner tonight."

Feeling bewildered by such munificence on the part of the Duke and at the same time a little shy of her appearance, Leona walked back along the corridor to the large room where she had met him on her arrival.

He was waiting for her and she thought there was a look of approval in his eyes as she moved towards him.

She curtseyed.

"I am overwhelmed, Your Grace, by your kindness. I only hope my appearance meets with your approval."

"You look very attractive," the Duke said, "and I expect there have been lots of men to tell you that before now."

Leona smiled.

"I have lived a very quiet life in the country and Mama had not been well this past year."

"No, of course not," the Duke said, "and that was why I was sure you would require many things which I hope I can provide for you."

"You are very thoughtful and generous."

"I want you to realise," the Duke replied, "that this is your home and that you will take your place in the Castle as if you were my daughter."

"But I thought you had a daughter!" Leona exclaimed, remembering that her mother had spoken of the Duchess having children.

"My daughter is dead."

"Oh . . . I am sorry!"

"She died two years ago. She was younger than you and never was strong."

There was a note in the Duke's voice which made Leona feel that he had suffered when his daughter died.

"I am so very sorry," she said again. "But you have other children?"

"I have a son."

Leona was about to ask if she would meet him when the Duke said:

"Luncheon is waiting for us and I feel that after your journey you must be hungry."

"Yes, I am, Your Grace."

Even as Leona spoke she remembered the cries of the children being evicted and felt as if food would choke her.

She wanted to speak of them to the Duke, to beg him to be merciful, to ask if any arrangements had been made to provide them with another home.

But then as they moved towards the Dining-Room she found it difficult to know what to say.

She was well aware that if she raised the subject he would brush it aside as he had done already. Yet she told herself she must not be a coward. Sooner or later she must talk to him about the Evictions.

It was, however, impossible to do so at luncheon.

She had expected to find herself alone with the Duke, but to her surprise there were a number of people waiting for them in the Dining-Hall.

It was an enormous Baronial Room, far larger than the Dining-Room at Cairn Castle, and the table could easily have seated thirty people or more.

They sat down eight for luncheon. The other guests were two elderly cousins who lived in the Castle, the Duke's sister, who was there on a visit, two neighbours who had been invited for luncheon, and a Minister from the fishing village which lay at the mouth of the river.

'Perhaps I will be able to talk to the Minister,' Leona thought as she was introduced to him.

But as the meal progressed she realised very clearly that the Minister was in considerable awe of the Duke and was prepared to agree with him on any subject under discussion.

She had the feeling that if it did not please the Duke, the Minister would not be prepared to offer the evicted families even the hospitality of his Churchyard.

However strongly she felt on the matter, Leona realised that nothing would be gained at this particular moment by upsetting the Duke.

She had seen the anger on his face and heard the coldness of his voice when she had first spoken of the Evictions.

"As Leona Grenville is to make her home with us," the Duke was saying to his cousins, "we shall have to see if there are any festivities or amusements in the neighbourhood, otherwise she will find Scotland a dull place."

"I assure Your Grace," Leona interposed, "where I lived in England it was very quiet, and I love the country, so please do not trouble about entertaining me."

She looked across the huge Dining-Hall at the sunshine outside the windows and went on:

"I want to find the white heather which my mother has always told me was lucky, and I hope that I shall see the salmon in the river and the grouse rising on the moor."

"I can promise you all those things," the Duke said. "Do you ride?"

"I love riding," Leona replied.

"You will find all the horses that you need in my stables," the Duke told her. "And for the moors there is nothing more sure-footed and hardy than the Ardness ponies, which are, I assure you, famous."

"I shall look forward more than I can possibly say to riding one."

Everybody was so kind to Leona and so pleasant that she thought she would be very ungrateful if she did not appreciate the efforts which were being made to welcome her.

At the same time, she could not help thinking of Lord Strathcairn and the way in which she had felt safe and protected when she was with him.

Perhaps it was the largeness of Ardness Castle, perhaps it was, despite his kindness, that she was afraid of the Duke, but there was something that made her feel nervous and a little ill at ease.

After luncheon the Duke asked if she would like to see the State-Rooms and he took her first to the Chief's Room, which, unlike the one she had seen at Cairn Castle, was on the ground floor.

It was, she thought, one of the largest and most impressive rooms she had ever seen.

"This is where our Clan gathered when we were attacked by marauding bands of hostile Clans," the Duke explained, "or when the Viking ships were sighted out to sea."

There was room, Leona thought, for hundreds of Clansmen and their families, and hanging on the wall were the trophies they had won in battle.

There was even a flag which had been captured from the English at the battle of Preston Pans.

"It is magnificent!" she said, knowing that the Duke expected her to comment on what she saw.

"This is the finest Chief's Room in the whole of Scotland," he answered, "and on the walls you will see the Coats-of-Arms of the families who have joined with ours down the ages. The Earldom goes back to the Twelfth Century, but the Dukedom is of fairly recent origin, and always the Chieftain of the MacArdns has been succeeded by his son."

"That is a wonderful record," Leona said. "And your son in his turn will succeed you!"

"He will!" the Duke answered.

He took Leona from the Chief's Room to various other places in the Castle where there were relics of the past, treasures that had been accumulated down the ages.

Then he opened a heavy oak door and she saw a flight of stone steps.

"This leads to the tower," he said. "I think it would interest you to see where my ancestors kept a man on watch day and night for fear of being surprised by the Vikings."

"And did they ever succeed in capturing the Castle?" Leona asked.

"Once, and they stayed here for two months," the Duke replied.

There was a faint smile on his lips as he continued:

"The legends allege that the reason why many of the Clan are so tall is that they have Viking blood in their veins, and there is no doubt that there are many

fair-haired MacArdns who appear more Scandinavian
than Scottish!"

"I noticed when I arrived that many of your servants seem to be very tall," Leona said.

"They are chosen for their height," the Duke
replied. "Shall I lead the way up the steps?"

"Yes, please do."

The Duke went ahead of her and the stone steps
spiralled up inside the tower with only arrow slits to
let in the light.

Another heavy oak door with wrought-iron hinges
opened at the top and as she stepped out onto the
top of the tower she had a view that was breathtaking.

Looking east, she could see miles out to sea;
north, there were high mountains silhouetted against
the sky; to the west, the deep dark Glen through
which she had journeyed to the Castle lay beneath
her.

It was all very beautiful and at the same time,
as she had thought before, awe-inspiring.

She looked first one way, then another. Then her
eyes rested on the small village almost directly below them where the river ran to the sea.

She could see the harbour with its stone walls
and one or two fishing-boats tied up beside the jetty.

"Is there plenty of work there?" she asked.

"There is always work for those who look for it,"
the Duke answered.

"But is it not only for people who have a knowledge of the sea and its ways?" Leona questioned.

She was thinking of the people who had lived up
the Glen. They would understand only how to till the
soil and feed cattle.

"I think you will realise," the Duke said, "that
from here a watcher would have plenty of time to
warn the Chieftain that an enemy was approaching
from whichever direction he came."

With an effort, Leona repressed the words which
had sprung to her lips.

She knew only too well that the Duke was aware

of what she wanted to say and had no intention of letting her say it.

Once again he had brushed her aside, and she knew it was impossible for her to go on speaking of the evicted people, however much she wished to do so.

Talking of the Vikings, explaining how they had brought their long boats up the river, the Duke would have been extremely interesting, Leona thought, if she had not all the time been conscious of the misery and unhappiness she had seen up the Glen.

She could not help thinking what a very long time it would take the women to walk all the way down to the sea carrying their children.

They might perhaps use a small cart for their belongings, but they would also have to drive what animals they possessed in front of them.

But what could she say? How could she help them?

She felt helpless as the Duke, having finished speaking of the Vikings, made her descend the stone steps in front of him so that he could close the door of the tower.

There were other things for her to see in the Castle, and because they had luncheoned late, it was tea-time long before Leona expected it.

The Duke took her into another Sitting-Room that was smaller and in a way more comfortable than the one in which he habitually sat.

Here his sister and the elderly cousins were waiting to give Leona tea, and they sat round a table in the centre of the room, on which was spread all the fascinating Scottish delicacies her mother had described to her so often.

There were griddle-cakes, baps, scones, bannocks, currant-bread, ginger-cake, shortbread, and many other items, of which Leona did not know the names.

"You are eating very little," the Duke's sister said to her. "You will have to get used to the large meals we all enjoy in Scotland. I think perhaps it is the fresh air which gives us such large appetites."

"I am sure it is," Leona answered.

At the same time, she wondered if she would not get very fat if she ate as much as everyone else seemed ready to do.

"I expect you would like to rest before dinner," the Duke's sister said when tea was finished.

"I would like to write a letter," Leona answered.

"You will find a writing-table in your bed-room," she was told, "and if there is anything you want, ask Mrs. McKenzie to procure it for you."

"Thank you."

Leona curtseyed politely to the others and went from the room.

She had a little difficulty in closing the door, and as she was doing so she heard the Duke's sister say:

"A very polite and charming young girl. I can understand why my brother was so pleased to have her here."

"Yes, she is delightful!" another lady remarked. "And how is Euan?"

"Very much the same," the Duke's sister replied. "But do not mention him to His Grace."

"No, of course not," was the reply. "I have been very careful not to do so after you warned me. . . ."

Leona shut the door.

She wondered who Euan was. Then as she walked along the corridor towards her bed-room she knew that she had seen the name somewhere, and then she remembered.

It had been written at the end of the family-tree hanging in the Chief's Room, which the Duke had shown her proudly.

It had in fact been extremely impressive, depicting the MacArdns all down the centuries branching out and marrying into the distinguished families of Scotland.

Then first the Earldom, then the Dukedom, descending from father to son, was chronicled until at the end there came the name Euan.

Leona knew that he was the Marquess of Ardn,

the title which was borne by the Duke's first-born son, and in this case, only son.

Now she wondered what was wrong with him, and if he was ill why his father should not be willing to talk about him.

It seemed a mystery, and she knew only too well how brusquely the Duke could set on one side a subject he did not wish to discuss.

"I shall find out about it in time," she thought.

Walking into her bed-room, she found that although she had not noticed it before there was a writing-table in front of one of the windows.

She sat down and, taking a sheet of heavy parchment, put it down on the blotter and dipped a quill in the ink.

"Dear Lord Strathcairn," she wrote.

Only to write his name was to bring him back vividly to her mind—his clear-cut features, his air of authority which was very unlike the overpowering manner of the Duke, and yet which told her that he was a leader, a man used to command.

She could recall the strange feeling that had been hers when they had looked into each other's eyes. It had made her feel a little breathless, and yet at the same time it had been exciting.

He had thought her beautiful and he had said he was always at her service.

She had an irresistible longing to see him and to talk to him again.

"Somehow I will get to Cairn Castle," she decided, and wondered if she dare ask the Duke to send her there in the carriage.

She had the inescapable feeling that he would refuse, and yet there was no reason why he should. After all, she was not bound by their feuds and disagreements of the past.

Then she asked herself if the feud was indeed a part of the past. Was it not very much of the present, and did it not involve the Clearances?

She wished that Lord Strathcairn had confided in her.

Why had he not told her what to expect? And why, she asked herself now, had he suddenly seemed cold and withdrawn from her when she asked him quite simple questions?

'Everything in Scotland seems so mysterious,' Leona thought, and she wondered again why the Duke's guests could not speak to him of his son.

The sheet of writing-paper was waiting in front of her and she wrote:

> Thank You so very much for Your Kindness to Me. First for the manner in which You saved Me after the Accident, and secondly for showing Me my first Glimpse of the Scotland my Mother loved. It was everything I had imagined—only even more marvellous.
>
> I shall always Remember the Beauty of Your Loch and the Music of the Pipes. It is difficult to put into Words, but I felt when I heard Them that I belonged and that Scotland called to my Scottish Blood.
>
> I would like Very much to meet Your Lordship again and I hope it will be possible. If I cannot come to you by Carriage, perhaps one Day I will be able to ride over the Boundary. In the meantime, My Lord, Thank You once again for so Much that I cannot Express in words.
>
> It was all very Wonderful for me.
>
> > I remain,
> > Yours Respectfully,
> > Leona Grenville

She read the letter through several times and felt that somehow it expressed very inadequately all she felt in her heart. Then she addressed it and rang the bell.

The maid, Maggy, appeared after a few minutes.

"Ye rang, Miss?"

"Yes, Maggy. I want this letter to go to the post, but I do not know how I should send it."

"Awl the letters are placed on the table in the Hall, Miss."

"Then would you be kind enough to place it there for me, Maggy?"

"Aye, Oi will, Miss."

The maid took the letter in her hand and then asked:

"Is there anything else, Miss?"

"I think I would like to rest," Leona answered. "When you have put the letter ready for the post, perhaps you would come back and undo my gown."

"Oi'll do that, Miss."

The maid disappeared and Leona saw that there was a bookcase in one corner of the room.

She selected a book that looked interesting and when Maggy returned to help her out of her gown she lay on her bed covered by a warm quilt and opened the book.

She was not really tired, but she felt in some way that the Duke's sister and the other ladies expected her to retire, perhaps so that they would not be put to the necessity of entertaining her.

'I am quite happy on my own,' Leona thought and opened her book.

She did not, however, read it.

Instead, she found herself wondering what Lord Strathcairn would think when he received her letter.

Had she been profuse enough in her thanks? Would he understand how very grateful she was for the kindness he had shown her?

"I must see him again! I must!" Leona murmured.

He had said that Cairn Castle was only three miles over the moors.

Perhaps she was being conceited—she might be quite wrong—but she had the feeling that possibly he would ride near the cairn which was his boundary, hoping he might see her.

'If only I could have stayed a little longer,' Leona thought.

Then she told herself that she was being very ungrateful.

The Duke had been overwhelmingly kind. He had given her these beautiful gowns and was going out of his way to make himself pleasant.

He had even spent so much time taking her round the Castle and up to the tower.

"Mama would be very thrilled to know that I am here," Leona told herself.

She had seen several portraits of the Duchess while going round the Castle. She had an expression of kindliness and compassion which somehow reminded her of her mother.

Leona could not help wishing that the Duchess were alive.

'We could have talked of Mama,' she thought.

She had a sudden longing for her mother that was almost a physical ache.

She wanted to tell her about Lord Strathcairn, she wanted to ask her advice about the Evictions, and she wanted her to reassure her that there was nothing frightening about the Castle.

"I am just being imaginative," Leona told herself, "but there is something . . . I know there is!"

She had often thought that her mother was fey, and in fact Mrs. Grenville had admitted that sometimes she knew with an inner conviction things that were not known to other people.

Then she would laugh to herself.

"Superstition is woven into the history of the Macdonalds," she would say. "When they lived in Glencoe they believed in moon-struck men who suddenly acquired lunatic powers, and in the great black cats that gathered to play mischief on All Hallows Eve."

Leona had been entranced.

"Tell me more, Mama!"

Her mother had laughed.

"The Macdonalds of those days believed in malevolent goblins in the hills, and by the willow and oak at Achnacore there were kindly fairies."

"I would love to have seen one!" Leona exclaimed.

"But when disaster was coming," her mother went on, "the Big Man walked at night by Ballachulish, the cows broke from the pasture and ran up the brae bellowing mournfully, and the voices of men about to die were heard crying in the darkness outside even though their bodies were still sitting by the fire!"

Leona had shivered, but she would press her mother to go on telling her of the superstitions in which the Macdonalds believed.

"There were men and women with the 'Evil Eye,'" Mrs. Grenville related, "and there were those who could see through earth and space and tell what was happening at that very moment beyond the mountains."

"And there were those who told fortunes?" Leona asked, knowing the answer but wanting to hear it again.

"There was an Oracle who could boil mutton from a shoulder blade and read the future in the markings on the clean bone."

"That is more exciting than the way the gypsies tell it with cards!"

"It was more truthful," Mrs. Grenville admitted, "but all believed in the 'Second Sight,' although it was wiser not to ask about the future, and no good came of it."

"I have no 'Second Sight,'" Leona told herself now, "but perhaps because I am half Scottish I am more sensitive to atmosphere than are other people."

Then she laughed at herself.

"It is just that I have a more vivid imagination!"

And yet she had known when Lord Strathcairn had held her in his arms that she could trust him and he would protect her from harm.

It had been, when she thought of it, a strange and very unlikely situation for a young girl to find herself staying alone at a Castle with a young man. Yet never for one moment had she been apprehensive or ill at ease.

But while she had felt like that at Cairn Castle, here at Ardness there was something frightening to which she could not put a name, but which neverthe-less was there.

Resolutely she forced herself to try to read her book.

Instead, she found herself listening to a silence that was broken only by the song of the birds outside the windows, and looking round the bed-room, which while large and luxurious was quite unexceptional.

"If only Mama were here," she sighed again, and thought that her mother would know what was trou-bling her.

Her fears however were forgotten when Mrs. Mc-Kenzie and the maids laid a bath for her and, after she had bathed, dressed her in one of her new eve-ning-gowns.

It was the loveliest gown Leona had ever pos-sessed.

The huge crinoline swung out from her small waist and she looked with delight at the frilled skirt and the bertha embroidered with diamanté and caught below her naked shoulders with tiny bunches of rose-buds.

"Ye look real fine, Miss!" Mrs. McKenzie ex-claimed. "I'm sure ye should be a-goin' to a Ball, not just to dinner wi' a lot of auld folk."

"It is the most beautiful gown I could ever imag-ine," Leona cried.

"His Grace'll be glad it pleases ye."

Leona walked a little self-consciously along the corridor, glancing at herself in the mirrors as she passed them.

She tried not to wish that Lord Strathcairn could see her as she was dressed now, rather than in the plain gown she had worn when she dined with him the previous evening.

She reached the top of the stairs and was just about to enter the Duke's Room, where Mrs. McKenzie had told her the guests were to assemble before din-ner, when she heard voices in the Entrance-Hall be-low.

She looked over the stone balustrade and saw the

Duke, resplendent in his evening-kilt, talking with the Major Domo who had escorted her up the stairs on her arrival that morning.

The Major Domo was showing the Duke something.

Leona was just about to turn away in case they should think she was prying, when she realised that what the man had in his hand was her own letter which she had written to Lord Strathcairn.

They were discussing it, but because they were speaking in Gaelic, Leona, whose knowledge of the language was limited, could not understand what they were saying.

But then as she waited, thinking it an impertinence that the Duke should be shown her private letter, she saw His Grace take it from the Major Domo, walk across the Hall, and throw it onto the fire burning in the big open fireplace.

For a moment she was too astonished to move or even to be certain that what she had seen had in fact happened.

But as the flames leapt to destroy the letter she saw the Duke turn towards the staircase, and as if instinctively she wished to protect herself Leona moved.

Silently and swiftly she hurried across the carpeted floor to enter the Duke's Sitting-Room before he himself reached the turn of the staircase.

She was trembling with anger, but at the same time it was tempered with a fear that had lain deep down inside her ever since she first saw the Castle.

She knew now what that fear was—a fear of not being able to escape, of being, to all intents and purposes, a prisoner.

Trying to compose herself, she went to the window to stand looking out towards the sea.

"You are early!" she heard the Duke say behind her.

"Yes, indeed, Your Grace."

With an effort she moved towards him to say:

"I am wearing another of the beautiful gowns you have given me. I do not know how to thank you adequately. I have never before possessed anything so elegant."

"I am glad it pleases you," the Duke said, "and it is certainly very becoming, but I think it needs one small addition."

"What is that?" Leona asked.

He drew something from the pocket of his evening-jacket and she saw that it was a small velvet box.

She took it from him automatically, her eyes worried.

"It is a present. I hope you will like it."

He spoke reassuringly, as he would speak to a nervous child.

Leona opened the box.

Inside was a pearl necklace, small but exquisite, the perfect ornament for a young girl.

"But I . . . cannot accept . . . this!" she exclaimed.

"It belonged to my wife," the Duke said, "and as she was so fond of your mother I feel that she would wish you to have it."

"It is . . . too kind, I . . . do not know what to . . . say," Leona stammered.

The Duke smiled and took the pearl necklace from the case.

"Let me put it round your neck."

As she turned her back on him obediently and bent her head, he fastened the clasp.

"Look at yourself in the mirror over there," he suggested.

She did as she was told and saw that he had been right in thinking it was the one thing necessary to make her appearance perfect.

The off-the-shoulder bertha revealed the whiteness of her skin, but now her softly rounded neck was encircled with the translucence of the pearls, and they gave her a touch of sophistication which she had not had before.

"Thank you . . . thank you again!" Leona cried. "But I do not know why you should be so . . . kind to me."

"There are plenty of reasons I could give you," the Duke answered, "but let me say for the moment that I want you to find happiness here at Ardness Castle."

"It would be difficult not to be happy in such circumstances," Leona answered.

But even while her lips spoke the words her brain was asking questions to which she could find no answers.

Why had the Duke burnt her letter? Why was no-one allowed to mention his son, Euan? And why, appearing to be so kindly, should he order such cruelties as the Evictions to be perpetrated?

Once again, there was no chance of her speaking of such things.

There were many more people for dinner than there had been for luncheon.

Leona found that there were quite a number of middle-aged and elderly men staying at the Castle who had been out grouse-shooting or fishing during the day and had returned eager to talk of the sport they had enjoyed.

To prevent the party from being too excessively male, several neighbouring ladies had been invited to dinner, who, Leona realised, stared at her with undisguised curiosity.

Once again the Duke explained that she was to make her home with him at Ardness Castle.

She thought, although she was not sure, that there was a speculative as well as a curious expression in their eyes as they looked at her.

She, however, enjoyed herself, simply because the elderly gentlemen were only too pleased to pay her compliments and to tell her about themselves.

The majority came either from the north of England or from the Lowlands of Scotland.

"We stay here every year," one of them said to

Leona, "and the shooting at Ardness is, in my opinion, better than anywhere else in the north."

As he spoke he bent forward to say to the Duke, who was several places away from him:

"By the way, Duke, those sheep of yours spoilt our sport today."

"They did?" the Duke questioned.

"They ran ahead of the line and put up birds before they were within shot."

"I will speak to my keeper about it," the Duke promised.

"I hope you will," the sportsman answered. "The sheep may mean money in your pocket, but they will not improve your game-bags."

The Duke did not reply and the man who had spoken, who was obviously an Englishman, turned back to Leona.

"The Landlords of the north are obsessed with sheep," he said. "But from what I hear there will be wool coming from Australia that will knock the bottom out of the Highland prices."

"In which case," Leona said in a low voice, "perhaps they will find it was a mistake to replace men and women with sheep!"

There was a note in her voice that made her dinner-partner glance at her sharply.

"You are thinking of the Clearances."

"I am indeed!"

"I read some articles about them in the *Times*, and thought it was a damned disgrace!"

"Surely something will be done?" Leona asked.

He shrugged his shoulders.

"What can those who live in England do? And from all I hear, there are more evictions planned in South Uist, Barra, and Skye."

"Oh . . . no!" Leona exclaimed. "Why cannot someone appeal to the Queen?"

The man to whom she was speaking smiled.

"Even the Queen has little authority over the great Scottish Landlords like our host," he said.

Then, as if he thought the subject had become embarrassing, he turned to speak to the lady on his other side.

'There is nothing I can do . . . nothing!' Leona thought.

She wondered whether if she persisted in expressing her opinions the Duke would be really angry and send her away.

He had been so kind to her that she ought to feel nothing but gratitude towards him.

Yet she now felt as if the gown she wore and the pearls round her throat were as treacherous as the thirty pieces of silver which Judas had been paid for betraying his Master.

After dinner was finished and the piper had encircled the table in the traditional manner, the ladies retired to the Drawing-Room, which was another magnificent Salon which Leona had not seen before.

Furnished, she learnt, by the late Duchess, it was very much more elegant than the other rooms, the furniture showing a French influence and the curtains and carpet being elaborate both in colour and material.

There were polished tables on which were arranged *objets d'art* which Leona was certain had been collected by the Duchess personally.

There were Georgian snuff-boxes set with enamel and jewels, Sèvres china, and some delightfully carved pieces of jade.

As she was examining some of them, one of the guests, who she had learnt was called Lady Bowden, came to her side.

"You look as if you were dressed especially for this room, Miss Grenville," she said pleasantly.

"Thank you for the compliment, Ma'am."

"We do not often find anyone so young and attractive at the Castle," Lady Bowden went on, "and the Duke tells me you are to make your home here."

"Yes, Ma'am. My parents are dead and my mother was a great friend of the Duchess Jean."

Lady Bowden sighed.

"We all miss the Duchess. She was a charming person, in fact she kept the place human."

Leona looked at her questioningly, and she smiled as she said:

"I always feel when we come here it is like going into the Ogre's Palace. Do you not feel that yourself?"

Leona laughed.

It was in fact very much what she did feel.

They were standing alone in one part of the room and Lady Bowden glanced over her shoulder and lowered her voice.

"The Duke has been very difficult locally since his wife died. Perhaps you will have a softening influence over him."

"I think it unlikely I shall have any influence at all," Leona answered.

"I suppose you are too young," Lady Bowden said almost as if she spoke to herself. "When he lost his daughter, Elspeth, I thought he would never smile again."

"Why did she die?" Leona asked.

"She was never very strong," Lady Bowden said, "and I think she did too much. She was only fifteen and because she adored her father she would go out shooting with him, she would ride with him, she expended all her energy in being the companion he had always wanted."

Lady Bowden paused.

"It was a very hard winter and she drove herself on when she should have been in bed. Her cold turned to congestion of the lungs, she developed pneumonia, and there was no hope."

"How sad!" Leona cried. "I can understand what His Grace felt."

"Of course it was worse for him than for anyone else," Lady Bowden said, "seeing that his son . . ."

She checked her words as the Duke's sister came across the room to ask:

"Are you going to play cards, Lady Bowden? You know how much His Grace enjoys a game of whist."

"I shall be delighted!" Lady Bowden replied.

She moved away from Leona towards the card-table as the door opened and the gentlemen joined the ladies.

'What had she been about to say?' Leona wondered.

It was infuriating that the sentence had not been finished and she had not learnt about Euan.

But there would be no chance of further conversation with Lady Bowden, as she was now sitting at the card-table and those who were not to play whist congregated round the fire.

"It is strange in this part of the world how cold it gets in the evening," someone remarked. "It was so hot on the moors today that I wanted to take my coat off."

"I suppose that is your excuse for having missed an easy right and left!" another man chaffed.

Then they were all talking sport and there was no chance of Leona learning more about the mysterious heir to the Dukedom.

Chapter Four

Leona had made up her mind that somehow she must cross the boundary to Lord Strathcairn's land and if possible see him.

She realised as the days passed at Ardness Castle that it was not going to be easy, for to begin with, whether this was by design or not, she never left the Castle unaccompanied.

The Duke, who seemed to be doing everything in his power to be pleasant and make her happy, took her riding, or she went driving with the other guests.

The first shooting-party left and another arrived, and there were large dinner-parties every night and always a dozen or more people to luncheon.

It seemed to Leona as if every moment of her day was filled with some activity or another, and she would have been extremely ungrateful if she had not been pleased and a little touched by the kindness that was shown her at every turn.

More gowns came from Edinburgh and with them were wraps edged with fur for the cold days ahead, and velvet jackets which it was still too warm to wear even when she was in a carriage.

She found it difficult to find new words with which to express her thanks to the Duke, but she felt almost as if he was watching her to observe her reaction to everything that happened and everything that was said.

And yet, however interested she was in the strange new life in which she found herself a participant, she could not help remembering a dozen times a day that Lord Strathcairn must think her impolite and very ungrateful.

She turned over in her mind ways by which she could write to him and thus replace the letter which the Duke had burnt.

Although she thought of asking when out driving if they could stop at a Post Office, she felt that the questions which would doubtless be asked would be an embarrassment, for she would then have to confess that she knew her first letter had not reached its destination.

However kind and pleasant the Duke might be, she knew she was afraid of him.

She was well aware that His Grace could be completely and utterly ruthless when it suited him, and there was no doubt in Leona's mind that everyone with whom he came in contact was in awe of him.

The servants rushed to do his bidding, and the local people whom she had met, like the Minister, were so obsequious and so humble in the Duke's presence that they made her feel embarrassed.

She wondered continuously what had happened to the families which had been evicted, but there was no-one from whom she could learn the truth.

It was impossible to question the Duke's servants about his actions, and she was sure that no-one else would have any idea what had happened or what would be the consequences of the Clearances she had seen taking place.

She searched the newspapers just in case there should be any more articles in the *Times* relating to what had happened in Ross.

After Mr. Delane's disclosures there had been formed a Society for the Protection of the Poor, but Leona gathered that its life had been brief, and of the moneys collected very little reached the Glencalvie people.

She did, however, learn from the newspapers

that there had been evictions at Glenelg and at Sollas on Lord Macdonald's land on North Uist. Others were taking place at Strathaid-on-Skye.

Very few details, however, were given of what had occurred, and Leona could only multiply in her imagination what she had seen on the Duke's land to know what the misery and cruelty was like.

"I must talk about it to Lord Strathcairn," she told herself a dozen times.

Then unexpectedly her opportunity came.

The Duke was asked to shoot with a neighbour on the other side of his northern border.

This meant, Leona learnt, that he would have to leave very early in the morning and would not return to the Castle until late in the evening.

It was, she told herself, the opportunity for which she had been waiting.

When Mrs. McKenzie called her, she looked out her bed-room window as the curtains were pulled to see if it was a fine day.

If it was pouring with rain, she was well aware, the shoot might be called off, or anyway the Duke might consider it injurious to his health to brave the elements.

But it was a perfect September day with a clear sky and a sun which would grow warmer as the day progressed.

Already the trees and shrubs round the Castle were beginning to show their autumn tints and the heather was in full bloom.

'Soon it will be winter,' Leona thought. 'Then I shall be really imprisoned here with no chance of escape!'

But today, whatever the consequences, she would, for a few hours at any rate, be free of the surveillance of the Duke.

She had her breakfast before any of the rest of the party were down and asked for a horse to be brought to the front door.

She was well aware that she would be accompanied by a groom, since it would cause far too much

comment and perhaps argument on the part of the
Major Domo if she said she intended to ride alone.

Wearing an extremely attractive new habit which
the Duke had had sent from Edinburgh, with a hat
encircled with a gauze veil, she thought as she took a
last glimpse at herself in the mirror that she wanted
Lord Strathcairn to see her as she was now.

He would remember her, she thought, in her
plain, cheap travelling-clothes which she had made
herself and which had none of the sophisticated *chic*
or elegance that the Edinburgh dressmaker had im-
parted to the garments she now wore.

"If he thought me beautiful then, what will he
think of me now?" she asked herself.

From the moment she awoke she had had an irrepressible feeling of excitement.

As she walked down the stone staircase to see
her horse waiting she felt as if her whole being had
come alive in a manner that was almost rapturous.

Only when she set out with the groom riding a
little behind her did she wonder if perhaps Lord
Strathcairn was away from home and after all her
planning she would be unable to meet him.

Then she told herself he had made it clear that
he was always there to protect and care for his Clan,
and he was not the type of Highland Landlord who
was attracted by the amusements and frivolities of
the south.

"He is everything Mama would admire," Leona
told herself, then had to admit that the Duke also
lived in his Castle amongst his people.

'But he does not care for them,' she thought
scathingly, 'it is money that matters most to him—not
human beings!'

She thought of the sheep she had seen roaming
over the moorlands, great flocks of them white against
the heather, and hated everything they stood for.

Then because for the moment it was difficult to
think of anything but Lord Strathcairn, she spurred
her horse into moving faster.

When they had left the drive of the Castle she turned south to climb the hill which she knew bordered the Strathcairn moors.

She rode up the side of it, being forced to move slowly because the ground was uneven and there were rabbit-holes into which her horse might stumble and strain a fetlock.

As she neared the top the groom drew even with her.

"Excuse me, Miss," he said in his broad Scots accent, "but ye're gettin' verra near tae the Strathcairn boundary, an' we're no allowed tae ride o'er it."

"I believe there is a cairn at the top," Leona replied. "I wish to see it."

"Aye, that there is," the groom replied.

As if having made an effort to restrain her, he had nothing more to say and dropped back. Leona moved on as quickly as she could, climbing all the time until the Castle lay beneath her.

It looked almost ferociously strong and impregnable in the sunlight.

The Glen beyond seemed dark and, as she had thought when she first drove through it, somehow ominous.

"There is something creepy about it," she told herself, then laughed to add:

"My imagination is running away with me."

It was difficult, with the freedom of the moors stretching in front of her and the sweet scent of the heather blowing in the wind, to remember her fears in the Castle!

How when she awoke at night she lay listening, although what she expected to hear she had no idea. How the shadows were often menacing.

Ahead of her she saw the cairn, great grey stones piled one on top of the other, and her heart leapt.

She knew that in a few seconds she would be on Lord Strathcairn's land.

She rode up to the cairn and pulled her horse to a standstill.

Then she looked to the south and saw first the Loch, then the Castle, as she had been longing to see them ever since she had left the beauty and peace of their protection.

The lights on the hills surrounding the Loch and its still water were even more beautiful than she had remembered.

The Castle in the distance had a fairy-like quality which made her think it had stepped right out of a book of fairy-tales which she had read as a child.

Her horse was no longer so frisky after the long climb and was content to stand still while Leona looked ahead and was reminded of the Promised Land of the Israelites.

She had thought of it and dreamt of it so often that she had been half afraid that when she saw it again it would have lost its magic.

But it was just as she remembered it, an enchanted stretch of water and an enchanted Castle.

She realised that the groom was fidgeting behind her, undoubtedly afraid of being reprimanded for having brought her up to the boundary, but she did not move.

She knew it would be ridiculous to imagine that Lord Strathcairn, after all this time without hearing from her, would expect her to appear now.

And yet, child-like, she had believed trustingly that he would be there.

'Dare I ride down in search of him?' she wondered.

She had the uncomfortable feeling that if she did so the Duke would be extremely annoyed; and yet, she reasoned, would he not be almost equally annoyed anyway when he was told she had ridden to the boundary?

"I might as well be hanged for a sheep as for a lamb!" Leona quoted to herself, and felt it was an apt adage.

She turned her horse's head and started to ride towards the Castle.

"Miss! Miss!" the groom cried agitatedly. "We're a-trespassing! This is Lord Strathcairn's Estate an' we shouldna cross the boundary!"

"I have been invited to do so," Leona replied, and continued to move forward.

The groom behind her was protesting beneath his breath in a manner which told her he was greatly perturbed.

She must have ridden for twenty minutes and the Castle was getting nearer, so that now she could see its turrets and the flag waving above the grey roof.

She could also perceive the small crofts nestling round the Loch-side, and she noted with satisfaction that there were no sheep on His Lordship's moors.

But as they rode they disturbed several large covies of grouse, the cocks cackling in indignation as they flew away to safety.

It was then that in the distance Leona saw a man on horseback and felt her heart leap.

She was not certain at first if it was indeed Lord Strathcairn, for the moors were undulating and after having seen him for a few seconds he disappeared out of sight, to reappear some minutes later.

Then she knew she had not been mistaken. It was Lord Strathcairn and he was coming towards her!

He was riding as fast as she was and now Leona touched her horse with the whip and she hurried forward, so eager to meet the man she was seeking that she was no longer concerned with her own safety.

The groom was still muttering and she knew that he was afraid that Lord Strathcairn would berate them for trespassing on his land.

But there was no disguising the gladness in His Lordship's expression when finally they came face to face.

"I had almost given up hope," he said as he drew his horse beside Leona's and held out his hand.

She put her fingers into his and he held them so tightly it was almost painful.

"You were . . . expecting me?" she asked in a low voice, finding it somehow difficult to speak.

"I have been watching for you every day since you left," he answered. "In fact one of my stalkers had a spy-glass on you from the moment you crossed the boundary."

It was what Leona had hoped and somehow expected, and yet it was an irrepressible joy to know that she had been right.

"I could . . . not come . . . before."

"Did you want to?"

There was something searching in the way he asked the question and because she felt shy she could not look into his eyes.

"I—I . . . wrote to you," she said, "but the . . . letter was never . . . despatched."

She saw his lips tighten, then he said:

"But you are here today."

"The Duke is shooting with a neighbour."

"Will you come to the Castle?"

"There is no need for me to be . . . back before . . . late this afternoon."

It was pointless, Leona thought, to pretend that she had not wished to see him.

Knowing that on her return she had to face unpleasantness, she might as well make the most of her escapade.

"You know how very welcome you are," Lord Strathcairn said.

There was a note in his voice that made Leona turn her head to smile at him; then, having met his eyes, she found it difficult to look away.

"Let us hurry," he said. "We have so much to talk about."

She knew he meant that what they said was best not overheard, and so they rode on in silence, the Duke's groom behind them, wondering, Leona was well aware, how much he would be blamed for what was occurring.

They reached the Castle and before the grooms

could hurry forward to help Leona from the saddle, Lord Strathcairn was there first.

He lifted her down and she felt a sudden thrill because his hands were touching her. She wished that he would carry her, as he had carried her once before, into the Castle and up the stairs.

But instead they ascended the staircase side by side to enter his special room which overlooked the Loch.

Leona went to the window and said:

"It is even more beautiful than I remember."

"And so are you!" Lord Strathcairn said quietly.

"Do you . . . really think so?" Leona asked.

"I really think so," he repeated with a smile.

"I am glad. I wanted you to . . . see me in my new . . . clothes."

Lord Strathcairn glanced at her hat and her fashionable habit as if he noticed them for the first time.

"Are they new?" he asked. "Your face is so lovely that it would be impossible for me to notice anything else."

She felt herself quivering and turned towards the Loch.

"So you have new clothes!" Lord Strathcairn said slowly, as if what she had said had just sunk into his mind. "Are they a present?"

"Yes . . . His Grace . . . gave them to me."

She wished now that she had not mentioned them, but she had wanted every time she wore a new gown for him to see her in it.

Lord Strathcairn moved from her side and crossed the room.

"Are you happy at Ardness Castle?"

"I . . . should be. The Duke is . . . extremely kind."

"That is not what I asked you."

"I know," Leona replied, "but it seems so ungrateful of me to complain when His Grace has given me so much and I have everything any girl could possibly need."

"Then what is wrong?"

Leona hesitated for a moment, until as if she could not help herself she said:

"When I left . . . here I . . . saw some of the Duke's . . . people being . . . evicted!"

She dare not look at him as she spoke, because she felt that the anger she knew he would feel would somehow react on herself.

Then he asked in an almost expressionless voice:

"Did it mean anything to you?"

"What would you expect it to mean? . . . It was something so . . . horrible, so degrading . . . so utterly inhuman . . . that it is difficult to speak of it . . . without tears," Leona replied.

There was a passionate note in her voice and her words seemed to vibrate round the room.

"And did you speak of it?"

"I tried to," she answered. "I swear to you, I tried to . . . but His Grace would not listen . . . and there was no-one else of whom I could even . . . enquire about their . . . fate."

Lord Strathcairn crossed again to her side.

"I am sorry you should have seen anything so horrible. But now perhaps you understand why the Duke and I are no longer on speaking terms."

"You are right! Of course you are right!" Leona said. "But what can be done?"

"Nothing!" he replied. "I have tried to help some of the MacArdns, but I cannot sacrifice the well-being of my own Clan by overcrowding the land."

"No . . . I can understand that," Leona agreed with a little sigh. "But those people! Those poor, wretched people! I can hear them crying now . . . and one child was nearly burnt to . . . death when they set fire to the . . . croft!"

"It is intolerable!" Lord Strathcairn said and his voice was harsh. "It is something which has happened all over Scotland—the greed of the Landlords and the cruelties of their Factors have crucified the Highlanders and destroyed the very souls of our people."

"I knew you would feel like that!" Leona cried.

"It is how my mother felt too! But is there nothing you can do?"

"Nothing!" he answered. "I have tried in every way I can. I have met a number of the Landlords and talked with them. We have held meetings in Edinburgh!"

He sighed before he continued:

"But already thousands upon thousands of Scots have been sent abroad and scattered all over the world. Fifty-eight thousand left in 1831 alone."

His voice was bitter as he finished:

"Now there is little land left which has not become a reserve for the sheep."

Leona could not speak. She knew that always at the back of her mind she had believed that Lord Strathcairn, like a Knight in Shining Armour, would be able to save the people from the Clearances.

As if he knew what she was thinking, he went to the grog-tray from which he had given her a lemonade the night she had stayed in the Castle and brought her a glass of sherry.

"We only have a little time," he said, "so let us resolutely talk of pleasanter things—yourself, for instance."

"But I want to talk about you," Leona protested. "I want you to tell me what you are doing here on your Estate. I want to hear about your plans for the people who are living in the crofts I can see round the Loch."

"Does it really interest you?" Lord Strathcairn asked.

"It really interests me," she answered. "I want to understand the problems of the Scottish people. I hate feeling isolated and that I am not a part of them even though I am living in Scotland."

"Is that how you feel at Ardness Castle?"

"It is full of people," Leona answered. "But they are guests. They come to the Highlands for amusement, but its problems are not theirs and they are not concerned."

"As you want to be."

"As I would . . . like to be."

There was a little pause and she had the feeling that he was looking at her speculatively. Then he said:

"Have you decided to make your home at Ardness Castle?"

"I have little choice," Leona answered. "I have no money, I have nowhere else to go, and the Duke is very anxious to keep me there."

Lord Strathcairn did not speak and she said:

"I only wish the Castle was more like . . . this."

"Where is the difference," Lord Strathcairn enquired, "except of course in the buildings themselves?"

"You know I was not referring to that," Leona answered. "The difference lies in the atmosphere. I suppose you will think it . . . foolish of me . . . but I somehow feel I am a . . . prisoner there."

She thought he looked startled, and he said sharply:

"Why should you feel like that?"

"I keep putting it down to my . . . imagination," Leona answered. "Or perhaps the spirits of the past still inhabit the great rooms, the long corridors, and of course the tower! But although I try to pretend otherwise, I am a little frightened!"

"I am sure it is not like you to be afraid."

"I do not remember ever being afraid before. But the place seems to be dark and secretive . . . and there is something . . . I only wish I knew what it was . . . which makes me afraid!"

She thought that she sounded childish and because she wished to change the conversation from herself she said quickly:

"Tell me about the Duke's son."

"Euan Ardn?" Lord Strathcairn asked. "He is not in the Castle?"

"No, I do not think so," Leona replied. "But everyone is very mysterious about him. I overheard the Duke's sister warning a lady not to mention him to His Grace."

"I believe he is in a Nursing-Home either in Edinburgh or in London," Lord Strathcairn said.

"But why?" Leona enquired.

"Nobody quite knows," he answered. "He was a sickly child, and I remember hearing that the Duke had taken him to various Specialists in Europe in the hope of finding a cure."

"A cure for what?"

"That is part of your mystery," Lord Strathcairn replied. "I do not know. In fact I think nobody knows."

He paused, then went on:

"I met the Duke's daughter, Elspeth, many times. She was a very attractive young girl and very like the Duchess, but I cannot remember ever having set eyes on the Marquess, nor has anyone else of my acquaintance."

"How strange!" Leona exclaimed.

"There have, of course, been all sorts of speculations as to what is wrong with him," Lord Strathcairn continued, "but I think it is generally believed that he has something wrong with his spine."

That would account, Leona thought, for the Duke going from doctor to doctor to find a cure, and obviously the boy had been given treatment in various European Spas.

"I can understand that it is a great disappointment to the Duke," she said aloud.

"Of course," Lord Strathcairn agreed. "He has always been excessively proud of his family."

"He is indeed," Leona smiled. "He showed me the family-tree. He also told me that the title had always passed from father to son and when he dies his son will inherit."

"That sounds as if young Euan is improving in health," Lord Strathcairn remarked.

"I think," Leona said, "that His Grace wants me to take the place of his daughter. Lady Bowden told me he was desperately unhappy when she died."

"If you are trying to make me feel sorry for the Duke," Lord Strathcairn said, "you will not be successful. I find him obstinate, pig-headed, and ruthless to the point of cruelty! In fact I disliked him as much as he dislikes me!"

Leona gave a little sigh.

"I am afraid that he will be very . . . angry that I have come here today to see . . . you."

"You say the letter you wrote to me was never despatched—why?"

Leona hesitated for a moment before she told the truth.

"The Duke . . . destroyed it. I saw him put it in the . . . fire when he did not know I was at the top of the staircase."

Lord Strathcairn rose to his feet.

"That is intolerable!" he said angrily. "But it is what I might have expected. If only you were staying with somebody else in the neighbourhood—anywhere, rather than at Ardness!"

"But that . . . is where I . . . am," Leona said in a small voice.

"And yet by a miracle for the moment you are here. It was very brave of you, and let me assure you I am exceedingly grateful."

"It is I who should be grateful to you. You saved me after the accident. I was so happy the night I 'discovered' Cairn Castle."

"That is what I hoped you were thinking, if you thought of me at all," Lord Strathcairn said. "But I was afraid . . ."

"Afraid?" Leona questioned.

"That you had forgotten me!"

"I could . . . never do that!"

Again their eyes met and something strange and at the same time wonderful passed between them.

He took a step towards her and she felt that he was about to say something momentous, when the Butler announced from the doorway:

"Luncheon is served, M'Lord!"

Lord Strathcairn glanced at the clock on the mantelpiece.

"We are eating a little early," he said, "but I thought there might be a number of things we could do this afternoon before you have to return."

"I am quite happy to agree to anything you have planned," Leona replied.

She went into the Dining-Room she remembered so well and which seemed so much nicer in every way than the great Baronial Hall at Ardness Castle.

Even though the servants were waiting on them, she and Lord Strathcairn could talk freely and there seemed to be so much for them to say.

But afterwards it was difficult to recall what they had discussed. She remembered only that the food was delicious and everything they talked about had a magic all its own.

But then, she thought, everything in the Castle was touched with magic.

After luncheon, it was a joy to talk to Mrs. Mc-Cray, and to find that the other servants remembered her and that the bed-room where she had slept was just as attractive as she recalled.

She thought that if she were sleeping once again in the Thistle Chamber she would not be listening as she did at Ardness Castle for sounds which never came, nor be lying awake, feeling afraid of the shadows for no reason that she could explain to herself.

"Have you been watching the dancing in the Chief's Room every night?" she asked eagerly.

"Not every night," Lord Strathcairn replied with a smile. "They usually gather on Saturdays, and once a month they bring their wives and children and their mothers and fathers, and give a demonstration of their skill."

"How I would like to see it!" Leona exclaimed.

"How I would like to show it to you!" Lord Strathcairn echoed.

They walked into the garden, and once again, Leona found that it was warmer than anywhere else, protected as it was by thick shrubs and walls, so that the flowers even in September were brilliant with colour.

Lord Strathcairn picked her a rose and she pinned it into the brooch at her neck.

She noticed he had chosen a white bud and she smiled as she remembered the white rosettes of the Jacobites. She mentioned this to him.

"Actually, I chose it because it is like you," he answered.

"A white rose?"

"White, pure, very beautiful, and still in bud!"

"And you . . . think that is . . . like me?"

"You give me the impression of being unawakened to life," he replied. "When you meet reality, like the Evictions, it hurts you because to you the world is still a wonderful place. And that is how it should be!"

"That is how I . . . want it to . . . be."

He did not speak and after a moment she said:

"You told me that one is often disappointed."

"But not always," he replied.

They wandered down to the edge of the Loch and she could see the water clear over the sandy bottom, small fish gliding in and out like transparent wraiths.

"Are there nymphs living in this Loch?" Leona asked. "And goblins burrowing under the hills?"

"But of course!" Lord Strathcairn answered. "And when I see the mists lying over the water in the morning it reminds me of you."

She turned to look at him and for a moment they were both very still. Then he said, as if it was a decision which was wrenched from him:

"I hate to hurry you, but I feel we should be getting back. Besides, there is something else I want to show you before we reach the boundary."

Leona felt that the sunshine was suddenly dimmed.

"I must not be . . . late," she said automatically, but in her heart she wanted to beg him to let her stay.

What did it matter if the Duke was angry? What did anything matter when she was at Cairn Castle with Lord Strathcairn?

If only she could stay there as she had done once before.

But she was far too shy to speak her inner thoughts, and walked beside him back to the Castle to put on her riding-hat and pick up her gloves and whip.

The horses were at the front door, the groom looking surly.

Lord Strathcairn lifted Leona into the saddle, then arranged her full riding-skirt.

She had a feeling that he did it in the same manner in which he had held her close against him, protectively.

There was a gentleness about him, she thought, that she had not expected to find in a man, and yet he was so essentially masculine.

He sprang onto his own horse and they moved away, the groom following some way behind so that he could not overhear their conversation.

"Did you really mean it when you said there was always someone watching the boundary?" Leona asked.

"I have instructed my stalkers that one of them must always be on duty," Lord Strathcairn replied. "I had a feeling they were beginning to give up hope and that they thought their vigil was a waste of time. Now they will watch more eagerly."

"So if I can . . . get away again . . ." Leona began.

"I shall be waiting," Lord Strathcairn said, "but I have been thinking . . ."

He paused.

"What have you been thinking?"

"That I should come to Ardness Castle and call on you."

Leona did not reply and after a moment he went on:

"You are very young and the Duke is in the position of being your guardian. I am very anxious to do nothing that will hurt you in any way, or that could possibly damage your reputation."

"How could you do that?" Leona asked in surprise.

Lord Strathcairn smiled.

"I think a large number of people, including the Duke, would think it very unconventional that you had stayed at my Castle and that you were alone with me today."

"Yes . . . of course," Leona said, a little dismally. "I had forgotten that."

"That is why I will call at the Castle with all pomp and circumstance," Lord Strathcairn said. "I see no reason, whatever the difficulties between His Grace and myself, why you and I should not start our acquaintance, perhaps a little late in the day, on the right foot."

He smiled as he spoke and Leona gave a little laugh.

"As you say," she said, "it is a little late in the day. I have stayed with you, I have spent a day alone with you, and . . ."

She stopped.

"I would like you to finish that sentence," Lord Strathcairn said insistently.

"I was going to . . . say that I have been so . . . very, very happy," Leona answered.

"And so have I!" he replied. "More happy than I can express in words, more happy than I should say at this moment."

Leona felt herself quiver at the meaning underlying his words and at the expression in his eyes.

They rode on in silence and now she could see the cairn ahead of them, the stones silhouetted against the sky.

She had a feeling that Ardness was waiting beyond it, reaching out its arms to drag her back into its very bowels, holding her so closely that she would never be able to escape a second time.

Then as the moor dipped down a small incline Lord Strathcairn drew his horse to a standstill.

"Do you mind walking to where there is something I wish to show you?" he asked.

"No, of course not," Leona answered.

He called up the groom and told him to take

charge of the horses. Then he lifted Leona from the saddle and taking her by the hand as if she were a child led her a short way across the heather.

They rounded a small hillock and there Leona saw a cascade bursting out from the side of the hill and tumbling in a silver stream into a small burn which twisted its way doubtless towards the sea.

"How pretty!" she exclaimed.

"It has been here for centuries," Lord Strathcairn said, "and it has a special secret that I wish to show you."

"How exciting!" Leona cried, but looking at the cascade she could not imagine what secret it could hold.

Lord Strathcairn walked ahead of her, drawing her by the hand to the very edge of the water until as he pushed aside the heather she saw that there was a narrow passage behind the cascade itself.

It was just wide enough for her to pass through without getting wet.

Now the water was thundering down on one side of Leona like a silver veil and as her eyes became accustomed to the darkness she saw there was a huge cavern going far back into the rock.

"A cave!" she exclaimed, and heard her voice echo a little eerily.

"This is where the Chief of the McCairns and thirty of his Clan hid after the battle of Culloden," Lord Strathcairn explained. "The English searched for them everywhere, even trying to burn down the Castle, but to all intents and purposes they had disappeared."

Leona moved a little further into the cave.

"How long did they have to stay here?"

"For three months! Somehow their wives and mothers managed to bring them enough food so that they did not starve, and when the English had gone they emerged safe and sound!"

"It is a perfect hiding-place!" Leona exclaimed. "How kind of you to show it to me."

"Even today very few people know of its existence," Lord Strathcairn said. "I need not ask you not to mention it when you are over the boundary?"

"You know I would never betray your confidence," Leona answered.

"I was sure of that."

He was standing with his back to the silver wall of cascading water, but Leona was facing it and the light of it was on her face.

"Now I shall think of you not only in the mists over the Loch," he said in his deep voice, "but also whenever I see a cascade or hear the music of it."

Their eyes held each other's.

Leona drew in her breath. Then without conscious volition, without thought, she moved towards him.

His arms went round her, and as instinctively she lifted her face, his lips came down on hers.

Leona had never been kissed before and she had not been warned what to expect.

Certainly not the little flame of fire that seemed to run through her veins and the sudden warm wonder which invaded her so that she felt as if she melted into him and became part of his very body.

She felt as if his lips took possession of her and she was no longer herself.

His kisses were part of the magic that she had felt at the Loch and at the Castle, and yet it was more bautiful and more intense.

The water falling beside them, its silver light which glinted in the air, and the strange, secret atmosphere of the cave itself were all in the insistence of his mouth.

It was as if time stood still; she was part of the history and wonder of Scotland and Lord Strathcairn embodied all the courage and manliness displayed by her childhood heroes.

He kissed her until the world no longer existed, until they were alone and the secret of where they stood was part of their hearts, their minds, and their souls.

Lord Strathcairn raised his head.

"I love you, my beautiful darling! I have loved you since the first moment I saw you!"

"I . . . love you . . . too!" Leona whispered. "It was because I felt so . . . safe in your arms that I wished . . . never to leave . . . them."

"My little love, I should never have let you go," Lord Strathcairn said. "I should have kept you with me. I should have held you."

His lips found hers again and he kissed her wildly, passionately, and possessively, so that she felt the little flame that had streaked through her at the first touch of his lips become a fire which invaded her whole being.

'I belong to him! I am his!' she thought triumphantly.

Then as he went on kissing her, she could think no more but only feel a rapture and an ecstasy that was part of Heaven itself.

"You must go, my darling," he said unsteadily.

"I cannot . . . leave . . . you," Leona cried.

It was sheer agony to know that he must stop kissing her. She wanted his lips more than she had ever before wanted anything in her whole life.

"We have to be sensible," Lord Strathcairn said. "I must look after you and see that we both behave with propriety."

"You will not . . . forget me?"

"Do you think that is possible?"

He held her close to him again and now he kissed her cheeks, her small chin, her straight little nose, then again her lips.

"Come, my precious," he said at length.

"I would like to stay here . . . with you for months . . . as your kinsmen . . . did."

"And do you suppose I would wish otherwise?" he enquired, and she saw the fire in his eyes.

With an effort he drew her to the side of the cave and, stepping out first, pulled aside the heather so that she could pass under the water unscathed.

The heather swung back into position and Leona

saw that it was impossible to see where they had been.

The sunshine seemed blinding and because she wanted so much to look at him again she dare not do so.

Because she longed for the touch of his hand she did not put her fingers into his.

Instead they walked back in silence and only when he lifted her into the saddle did she look down into his face and see in his eyes an expression which made her feel as if once again he kissed her lips.

She knew he was loving her as she loved him, but the groom was within hearing, and the horses moved over the heather towards the cairn.

Leona felt despairingly that there was only a few seconds left before they must part and she must go back to the darkness of the Castle.

They reached the cairn and she looked down into the Glen and felt herself shudder.

"It will not be long, my darling," Lord Strathcairn promised almost beneath his breath, "but if in the meantime you need me, you know you have only to stand here beside the cairn."

"You know I will . . . come if I . . . can."

"And you know I will come to you."

For a moment they looked into each other's eyes and it was with the greatest difficulty that Leona did not bend towards him so that he could kiss her lips.

But he lifted her hand, and regardless of whether the groom could see or not, he pulled back her glove at the wrist and kissed the little blue veins just below the palm.

She felt herself thrill at his touch and he knew that she quivered with a sudden ecstasy.

"Always remember that I love you," he said very sotfly.

Then as if he could not bear to see her go he turned and rode away in the direction of his Castle.

Leona watched him for a few minutes, then she began the descent down from the cairn towards the Glen.

saw that it was impossible to see more than a few
feet ahead the swirling snow that blinded him, and because
it was impossible to keep their eyes on the snow...

Chapter Five

Every moment that took her nearer to the Castle
made Leona feel more and more apprehensive.

At the same time, the glow of happiness within
her heart made her feel that the whole world vibrated
with joy.

"I love him! I love him!" she told herself.

With a sudden sense of rapture she raised her
face towards the sky to thank God for having brought
Lord Strathcairn into her life.

The wonder of his kiss and the ecstasy of knowing that he loved her made her feel braver than she
would otherwise have felt, but at the same time she
could not help feeling afraid of what lay ahead.

The Castle was grimmer and more awe-inspiring
than ever as she crossed the bridge over the river and
it loomed high above her. The windows seemed to be
eyes looking at her with disapproval.

She was well aware that a feud between Clans
was something which could be erased only in blood,
and even then the hatred would continue century after century, as violent and unrestrained as on the day
when it had first been aroused.

But this was not so much a feud between Clans
as a personal enmity between two men.

She could imagine how incensed the Duke would
have felt at having his actions challenged by somebody as young and to his mind as unimportant as
Lord Strathcairn.

Yet, man to man, Leona thought that Lord Strathcairn shone with the light of an avenging Angel, while the Duke was undoubtedly an Ogre whom he should vanquish.

"The Ogre's Castle!"

The description came to her mind as she dismounted at the great iron-studded door and the grooms took her horse.

She walked in to find the Major Domo waiting for her and she had the idea, although it might have been her imagination, that he was looking at her in a disapproving manner.

"What I do is not the business of the servants," she told herself proudly, and she walked up the stairs with her head held high and her back very straight.

She was well aware that the fact that she had crossed the boundary would already be known in the Castle.

The stalkers would have reported it. The gillies on the river and the keepers on the moors would undoubtedly have watched her and the groom riding up the hill and disappearing when they reached the cairn.

Such a bit of gossip would have run like wildfire through the Castle and perhaps by now it had even reached the chattering women in the fishing-village.

It was easy to understand how fast such a piece of information could travel when one thought of how the Fiery Cross had gathered a Clan when their Chieftain needed them.

Her mother had explained to her how two burnt, or burning, sticks were tied with a strip of linen which was stained with blood, and the cross was passed from hand to hand by runners in relays.

"One of the last occasions on which it was sent," Mrs. Grenville said, "was when Lord Glenorchy, son of the Earl of Breadal Bane, rallied his father's people against the Jacobites in 1745."

"Were they scattered over a large area?" Leona asked.

"The cross travelled about thirty miles about Loch Tay in three hours," Mrs. Grenville replied.

She smiled as she went on:

"A Clan which had been gathered by the cross was influenced by many superstitions—for instance, if an armed man was seen by the way, that was a portent of good fortune and victory."

"And what was bad luck, Mama?"

"A stag, a fox, a hare, or any other game that was seen and not killed, promised evil," her mother replied.

Her eyes looked back into the past as she said:

"I was always told that if a bare-footed woman crossed the road before the marching men, she was seized and blood was drawn from her forehead at the point of a knife!"

Strange superstitions, Leona thought now, and felt herself shiver because just before she reached the Castle she had a seen a magpie.

"They may not believe that one magpie brings sorrow in Scotland," she told herself.

As she reached the top of the steps she could not help wishing that she had seen two, which meant joy.

Then resolutely she gave herself a mental shake.

"I am being absurd! What can the Duke do to me? He is not my legal guardian, and since I take my father's nationality I am English!"

At the same time, she knew that her Scottish blood would not let her ignore the fact that she had broken the rules of the Chieftain who had appointed himself her guardian, and, as far as he was concerned, had fraternised with the enemy.

It was with a ridiculous sense of relief that Leona, when she reached the Drawing-Room where the Duke's sister was waiting for her, found that the Duke had not yet returned.

"We were worried about you, dear," the Duke's sister said. "My brother did not tell me last night that you also would be away today."

"It was rude of me, and I must apologise," Leona

answered, "but I did in fact expect to be back in time
for luncheon."

"Well, you are here now," the Duke's sister said
with a smile, "so we need not trouble His Grace with
my anxiety."

"I would not wish to . . . worry him," Leona answered.

At the same time, she was quite certain that as
soon as he entered the Castle the Duke would be
told where she had been.

She went to her room and lay down before dinner, but it was impossible for her to sleep.

All she could think of was Lord Strathcairn's eyes
looking into hers and the wild wonder he had aroused
when he kissed her until she could no longer think,
but only feel she was in a special Heaven where
there was only love.

"Love is divine!" she told herself.

She knew that nothing in the world could stop
her loving him, and that they belonged to each other
already as closely as if they were already united in
marriage.

'I shall live in that happy, beautiful Castle,' Leona thought. 'I shall look out onto the Loch. I shall
help to tend and protect the people who shelter beside it, knowing that their Chieftain will never betray them.'

It was at luncheon that Lord Strathcairn had
said to her:

"Leona is a very beautiful name. I have never before met someone who was called Leona."

She had blushed a little as she replied shyly:

"It seems somehow remiss of me, but I have never
heard your Christian name."

"It is Torquil," he replied. "The name goes back
far into antiquity. Many of my predecessors who were
called Torquil have performed feats of valour."

"Tell me about them," Leona begged.

He had related deeds of heroism performed in
war, affairs of honour when the Chieftain represented
the whole Clan, and ancient legends which invested

those named Torquil with almost supernatural powers.

Leona had listened with glowing eyes and felt that the name became him.

"Torquil!" she whispered to herself now, then aloud, as if the words burst from her she cried:

"I love you! Oh, how much I love you!"

She felt that her words winged their way across the moors towards him as if carried on the wind.

She had a feeling that he was thinking of her at that very moment, in fact she was sure he was.

"Love has made me fey," she told herself, "and because of it I can project my heart through time and space to him, and he will understand."

All too quickly Mrs. McKenzie and the maids arrived with Leona's bath and she knew it was nearing the time for dinner.

Now she must face the Duke and she was thankful that they were not to be alone. The Duke's sister would be there, although she had the idea there would be no-one else.

She was correct in this assumption; for one of the reasons the Duke had gone to shoot with a neighbour was that there were to be no guests on his own moors that day.

The house-party had in fact departed in the morning after Leona had left the house, but she only realised this from the conversation between the Duke and his sister over dinner.

She was aware that he did not address her directly and she was conscious that he was angry even before they proceeded into the Dining-Hall.

But he said nothing and Leona ate in silence while the servants presented the food on silver-crested dishes.

Even a profusion of candelabras on the table seemed not to illuminate the dark shadows in the corners of the great Hall.

The piper had chosen to play laments and dirges that evening, and by the time dinner was finished she felt as if she had sunk in stature and was so insignificant as to be almost invisible.

'Perhaps the Duke is so angry that he will send me away,' she thought.

Then she realised that, if he did so, she would simply go straight to Cairn Castle, where Torquil would be waiting for her.

She felt her heart leap at the idea and now her chin was raised a little higher. She told herself that as a Macdonald she need not be afraid of a Mac-Ardn, however imposing he might appear.

But when the Duke told her that he wished to speak to her in his room and his sister said good-night, Leona was well aware that her hands were trembling.

There was also a distinct and unpleasant feeling fluttering within her breast.

"Butterflies!" her mother had called them once, but Leona thought they were more violent than that lovely and colourful insect could ever be.

The door was shut behind the Duke's sister and His Grace walked slowly to the fireplace to stand with his back to the burning logs while his eyes rested on Leona.

He did not ask her to sit down and she remained standing, aware that the full skirts of her crinoline were moving a little with what was now a trembling of her whole body.

"I understand that you rode off my land today," the Duke began slowly.

"Yes . . . Your Grace."

"You did not inform me yesterday that you intended to do so."

"I made up my . . . mind at the . . . last moment . . . Your Grace."

"You wished to visit Strathcairn?"

"Yes, Your Grace."

"Why?"

"I wanted to thank him for his hospitality to me after the . . . accident, and I also wished to . . . see him."

"Why did you wish that?"

"He has become . . . a friend, Your Grace."

"A friend of whom you know I would disapprove!"

"I am not . . . concerned, Your Grace, with feuds or . . . disagreements which arose before I . . . arrived in Scotland."

"But you knew I would disapprove?"

"You had not spoken of it . . . but I had the . . . idea that Your Grace would perhaps not be best . . . pleased."

"You are at least truthful."

"I . . . try to be, Your Grace."

Leona wished that he would ask her to sit down because she was genuinely frightened that her legs would no longer support her.

Although the Duke was speaking in a controlled, almost unemotional voice, she could feel his anger vibrating from him and it was impossible not to be over-awed by his very presence.

He seemed to fill the whole room, and as she waited for him to speak again she felt he must hear her heart beating.

"You are quite right in thinking I would not approve of your friendship, if that is what it is, with Strathcairn," the Duke said after a moment. "I do not intend to give you any reasons why I do not consider him a suitable acquaintance for someone who is under my protection, but you will obey me when I tell you you are not to see him again!"

"I . . . I am afraid I . . . cannot agree to that, Your Grace."

Leona tried to speak firmly, but her voice sounded weak and ineffectual even to herself.

"Why not?"

"I . . . like Lord Strathcairn, Your Grace."

"*Like* him?"

The Duke's voice rose and he seemed almost to roar the question.

"I suppose you imagine that you are in love with him?"

Leona did not answer and after a moment the Duke said:

"I presume he has told you about his wife?"

"His . . . wife?"

Leona could barely whisper the words.

"Yes—his wife!" the Duke answered. "He is married to a play-actress, who does not live with him but who nevertheless bears his name."

For a moment Leona thought she would faint, then as she clenched her fingers until the nails hurt the softness of her palms, she asked in a whisper:

"Is . . . this . . . true?"

"Of course it is true!" the Duke retorted. "But I am not surprised that Strathcairn kept you in ignorance of what is undoubtedly a blot on his family escutcheon."

Without waiting for permission, Leona moved towards the nearest sofa and sat down.

She felt as if the ceiling had descended on her head and darkness had risen from the floor to engulf her.

It could not be true!

What the Duke had said must be a lie, and yet Lord Strathcairn had not spoken to her of marriage.

He had said that he loved her. He had drawn her very heart from her body and made it his, but he had never asked her to be his wife.

Now she could understand. Now perhaps she knew the reason why he had said he must protect her reputation.

What in fact could be more reprehensible than to be alone with a married man, to fall in love with him, to give him her lips, her very soul, when he belonged to someone else?

The emotions she was feeling must have made her look stricken and very pale, for the Duke pulled the bell violently. When the Major Domo appeared, he ordered brandy.

It was brought in a very few minutes in a cut-glass decanter on a silver tray on which there were crystal glasses.

The Major Domo would have poured it out, but the Duke waved him away and when the door was closed he half filled a glass and handed it to Leona.

"N-no . . . thank you," she tried to say.

"Drink it!" he commanded. "You have had a shock."

Because she felt too weak to argue with him, Leona did as she was told.

She felt the fiery liquid burn its way down her throat, and although she hated the taste of it she knew it cleared her mind and she was not trembling so violently.

The Duke took the empty glass and set it back on the tray.

"And now, Leona, I wish to talk to you."

She wanted to tell him that she could not listen, she wanted to run to her bed-room, to hide her unhappiness and the feeling that she had been betrayed.

But because the Duke's will was stronger than her own, she raised her eyes to his face and forced herself to attend to what he was about to tell her.

"I intended to wait a little longer," he began, "before I told you of my plans for your future."

Leona did not speak and he went on:

"I wanted you to feel at home here in the Castle. I wanted you to get acclimatised to our way of life."

"Y-Your . . . Grace has been very . . . kind," Leona managed to murmur.

It was difficult to speak, since all she was conscious of was a hard lump in her breast, as if someone had set a stone there.

"I had the idea," the Duke continued, "that we were making you happy. You are certainly different in appearance from when you arrived."

"I . . . have told Your Grace how . . . g-grateful I am for my gowns," Leona stammered, "and for the p-pearl necklace."

"They are only a part of all I wish to give you," the Duke said, "because I decided before you arrived, Leona, that you were the girl I was looking for to be my daughter-in-law!"

For a moment Leona thought that she could not have heard him aright. Then as her eyes questioned what he had said, the Duke repeated:

"I intend you to marry my son, the Marquess of Ardness!"

"But . . . why should you have . . . chosen me?"

"Because I admired your mother. You come from good Scottish stock. You are strong and healthy and you will, I believe, give my son an heir to the title, so that our family may continue in the direct line."

Leona clasped her hands together.

"But . . . I have not . . . met the Marquess, Your Grace."

"I am aware of that, and before you meet him I want you to understand exactly what such a marriage will entail as far as you are concerned."

He paused before he continued:

"You will live here, but there is also a family Mansion in London, a house in Edinburgh which is finer than Hollyrood Palace, and many Castles and properties in other parts of Scotland and on the Isles."

The Duke paused.

"You will be able to go abroad, Leona, and travel —something, I understand, you have never been able to do in the past. You can visit France and Italy. You can see the glories of Greece, and if it pleases you I shall be prepared to send you to other parts of the world."

Leona looked at him wide-eyed.

"And . . . your son. Has he been . . . consulted on this . . . matter?"

"Euan will marry you because I tell him to," the Duke said. "But I am going to speak frankly, Leona, and tell you that you need not concern yourself to any great extent with your husband once you have given him an heir."

"But why? I do not . . . understand! I was told that he was sick . . . but . . ."

"He has never been strong," the Duke interrupted, "and I have taken him to doctors all over the world. But doctors are fools! However, he is now a man and capable of breeding a child. That is all that need concern either of us!"

The Duke spoke almost roughly and Leona said:

"I am . . . sorry to sound foolish, but I still do not . . . understand. Why should the Marquess want such a . . . strange and . . . unnatural marriage?"

"I want you to marry him, Leona," the Duke said. "You are everything that I admire in a woman— everything that I have wanted in the mother of the future Duke."

"I am . . . honoured, Your Grace. At the same time, you will understand that I could not . . . marry a man I did not . . . love."

Even as she spoke she thought wildly that she would never love again, in which case she would never be married.

"That is the romantic idealism of a very young girl," the Duke remarked.

He rose to his feet to stand once again in front of the fire.

"You are intelligent enough to be aware that marriages in aristocratic families are always arranged. It is not a question of some sickly, sentimental emotion between two people who are too young to know their own minds, but an amalgamation of money and property between two families in whose veins runs the same type of blood."

"I have no . . . property, Your Grace. In fact I am penniless! And I should not have thought my blood the . . . equal of yours."

"Your father was an English gentleman and his antecedents are nothing to be ashamed of," the Duke said sharply. "Your mother was a Macdonald and your great-grandfather was a Chieftain of whom the Bards still sing."

Leona knew this was true but she was surprised that the Duke should be aware of it.

"I am therefore proud that you should bear the MacArdn name," he went on, "and when I die you will be the Duchess of Ardness!"

There was something so positive in his tone that it made Leona say hastily:

"Your Grace will . . . understand that I would like time to . . . think over your . . . suggestion."

"Think?" the Duke questioned. "What is there to think about? I have arranged your marriage, Leona, and it will take place tomorrow, or perhaps the day after."

"No . . . no!" Leona cried.

She felt that a tidal wave was sweeping her away and she was drowning beneath the force of it.

"I had meant, as I told you, to wait a little longer," the Duke said. "But by your action today you have precipitated things to the point when I can no longer play about with something which is of such paramount importance to me."

"But how can I be . . . married so quickly?" Leona asked. "It is impossible! Besides . . ."

Her voice died away.

She was about to say that she loved someone else, when she remembered that in any case she could never see Lord Strathcairn again, nor speak to him.

He had deceived her and she thought wildly that he had stolen her heart under false pretences.

I love you, my beautiful darling!" he had said. "I have loved you since the first moment I saw you!"

But he was a married man!

He had no right to love anyone but his own wife.

While he had talked of looking after her and seeing that they both behaved with propriety, he was behaving in such a reprehensible manner that even to think of it was as if a dagger pierced her breast.

He was another woman's husband—she knew that to love him would be a sin which offended every instinct of decency and honour with which she had been brought up.

So what did it matter what happened to her now?

If the Duke wanted her to marry his son it might be better than yearning for a man who was unworthy of what she offered him.

As if he knew the conflict which was taking place within her, the Duke said:

"Shall we look at the alternatives, Leona? If you will not marry Euan, then what will become of you?"

She made a little helpless gesture with her hands and he went on:

"It would be embarrassing for you to stay here. In any case, I will be frank and say I should find someone else to take your place. That would mean you would have to find employment and, although you are very beautiful and very charming, I doubt if you are skilled in anything that would be of value to the commercial world."

He paused before he said in a different tone:

"As the Duchess of Ardness you would hold a position in Scotland that is second to none. In England you would be welcome at Court. You would be fêted and acclaimed and your beauty would have the frame it deserves."

Again he waited for Leona to speak, but she was looking down at the ground, her eye-lashes very dark against the pallor of her cheeks.

"I think there is only one answer to my proposition," the Duke said. "It will be a very quiet wedding. In fact there will be no-one present at the ceremony except for the Minister and myself."

"I . . . I could not . . . marry anyone I had not . . . met beforehand."

An idea came to Leona that she must play for time.

Again she had the frightening feeling that she was being swept away on a tidal wave and she knew that the Duke was over-riding her, compelling her to do as he wished.

It was only because she felt so bewildered and stricken by the news that Lord Strathcairn was already married that she knew she had no strength with which to resist the Duke.

'I must not . . . allow this to happen,' she thought.

And yet it was happening, and she felt as though nothing she could say or do could stop the course of events.

"I had a feeling," the Duke replied, "that you would ask to see my son. It is in fact possible for you to do so at once."

Leona sat upright, startled.

"You mean . . . he is here?"

"He is in the Castle and has been for some years," the Duke answered. "But I keep it a secret because he has not been well."

His lips tightened and he said with a sudden bitterness in his voice:

"It seems impossible that I, who have never known a day's illness, should have fathered a weakling, but it is a cross that has been laid upon me."

For the first time Leona realised that the Duke was indeed suffering, and she began to understand what it had meant to him, with his pride in his family, to be inflicted with a son who was apparently an invalid.

"It is not just a question of inheritance," the Duke went on almost as if he spoke to himself. "As you are aware, a woman in Scotland can inherit, and it has often happened that the daughter of a Chieftain has carried on the Clan. But Elspeth died."

Leona's heart was touched.

"I am so . . . sorry for you."

"There are cousins of course to take my place," the Duke continued, "But they are not of my own flesh and blood. The hereditary line, as you saw for yourself on our family-tree, has been handed down from father to son for hundreds of years."

Once again his voice changed and there was a beseeching note in it as he said to Leona:

"Give me a grandson of whom I can be proud! Give me an heir to my title, a Chieftain of the Mac-Ardns, and everything I possess, everything you could desire, is yours!"

Leona knew that if she had never met Lord Strathcairn it would have been impossible for her not to respond generously to the appeal in the Duke's voice.

But despite what she had learnt, despite the hor-

for she felt in knowing he had betrayed her, some part of her was still his and the thought of another man touching her made her shiver as if at the touch of a reptile.

"Perhaps your son and I could . . . meet and get to . . . know each other?" she faltered.

The thought came to her that perhaps the Marquess wished to marry someone else, someone of whom the Duke did not approve, and therefore they could come to some understanding.

'If the Marquess and I could be friends,' she thought, 'if we could understand each other's feelings, then perhaps it would not seem so horrible.'

"As he is in the Castle," she said aloud with sudden resolution in her voice, "may I . . . please meet your . . . son?"

"I have already arranged that," the Duke said. "You see I am fey where you are concerned."

Leona looked at him in surprise.

It was somehow the last attribute she would have imagined in the Duke.

For the first time she thought of him as an ordinary man, sorrowing over his children without a wife to comfort him and help him bear the many responsibilities of his position.

'I must try to do what is right,' she thought.

She tried to forget the frozen weight within her breast and to ignore the knowledge that her whole being was crying out despairingly for Lord Strathcairn.

'I want him! I want him!' she cried within her heart as the Duke led her from the room and along the wide corridor.

'A married man!' her brain jeered at her. 'A man who belongs to someone else! What about the ideals in which your mother believed and which have been yours since you were a child?'

The Duke walked the whole length of the corridor on the first floor, and Leona realised they had reached another part of the Castle which she had not been shown.

The Duke unlocked a heavy door and they passed through it.

There were rooms opening off a small corridor with a window at the end of it.

He opened a door on the left and they entered a room that was lit only by candles and not very many of them.

There was however a bright fire in the fireplace, and as they entered two men rose to their feet.

For a moment Leona found it difficult to look at them because she was afraid, then she saw that one man was much taller and bigger than the other.

Because he was wearing a kilt, a very impressive sporran, and the usual silver-buttoned jacket, she knew he was the Marquess.

Automatically she followed the Duke across the room towards him.

"Good-evening, Euan!" she heard the Duke say. "I have brought Leona with me as I promised you. She is very pretty. Say good-evening to her, Euan."

There was silence. Leona curtseyed automatically and raised her eyes.

It was difficult in the candlelight to see anything except that the Marquess was very tall.

His face seemed a blur before her eyes. Then almost as though he were instructing a child, the Duke said again:

"Say good-evening to Leona, Euan!"

"Pretty—Leona—very—pretty!"

The words were spoken singly, took a long time in the saying, and were slightly slurred.

For a moment the idea flashed through Leona's mind that the Marquess was drunk. Then she looked at him more closely.

He had a large egg-shaped head, the hair receding from a high forehead. His eyes were small but protuberant and too close to his nose. His lips were thick, and his large mouth hung open.

Then Leona understood.

He was not drunk—he was abnormal! Retarded!

She had seen boys like him before. There was one in the village where they had lived. Not a loony, not mad to the point when he should be put away, but abnormal, with a brain unable to function in an abnormally large body.

As she realised the truth, she wanted to scream and as she fought for self-control, the Duke said:

"Give Euan your hand, Leona."

She was too bemused to disobey him, and put out her hand. The Marquess stretched forward to take it in both of his.

"Pretty—Leona! Pretty!" he said again, and now he was peering into her face. "Wife—wife for—Euan!"

There was a note of triumph in his voice.

"Pretty—wife—Leona!"

His hands were hot and his skin was soft, and yet Leona knew he had a strength which frightened her.

She tried to pull her fingers away but was unable to do so.

The other man who had been standing in the shadows came forward.

"That is enough, M'Lord!" he said sharply. "Leave go!"

It was a voice of authority and almost reluctantly, it seemed to Leona, the Marquess did as he was told and she was free.

But she felt that she was going to faint.

As if the Duke was aware of it, he put his hand under her arm and turned her towards the door.

"Good-night, Euan," he said. "Good-night, Dr. Bronson."

"Good-night, Your Grace."

Afraid that her feet would not carry her, yet somehow moving automatically at the Duke's insistence, Leona found herself in the corridor outside.

Then, as the Duke shut the door behind them, she heard a sudden cry.

"Leona—pretty—Leona! Bring her—back! I—want—her! I—want her!—I want—"

The door of the wing was shut behind them and there were no more sounds.

Leona sank against the Duke and he put his arm round her.

"Come, you have had a long day and it is time for bed."

She found it impossible to reply, and he half carried her along the passage to the door of her own room.

The lights were lit, but there was no-one there.

He took her to the bed so that she could sit down on it.

"My son is a little excited tonight," he said in a conversational tone. "He was told you were coming and that you are to marry him. Usually he is very quiet and extremely obedient."

"I . . . cannot . . . marry . . . him!" Leona protested weakly.

She forced the words through her lips and wondered if the Duke had heard them.

"You will feel differently in the morning," he said. "I have pointed out the alternatives. I have made it quite clear, Leona, that once you have fulfilled your part in producing a child, you need never see your husband again. I am told that those who are afflicted in such a manner do not live to be very old."

He paused and said:

"You are young and beautiful and you will be rich and powerful. I do not need to be fey to know there will be many men in your life. Men who will love you and to whom doubtless you will give your heart. There will be nothing in the least reprehensible about it."

Leona did not answer. She felt as if she were stricken by dumbness, as if her whole body were paralysed.

"Be sensible about this," the Duke said. "It would be a mistake to think about it for too long. In fact I am sure it would be in your best interests if you were married tomorrow night!"

His hand was on the bell-pull as he spoke, and without waiting for the maids to appear he went from the room.

* * *

It was very quiet in the darkness and Leona felt herself listening as she had done so often since she came to the Castle.

In the hours that had passed since going to bed, she felt as if a battle had taken place within her which had depleted her strength and in some horrible manner changed her very personality and character.

On the one hand, her whole being was weeping because of her love for Lord Strathcairn; on the other hand, she shrank in horror and disgust from the poor creature whom the Duke must call his son and whom he intended to be her husband.

Her mother had told her that such people were to be pitied.

"Few people understand any form of mental illness," she had said often enough. "In London, lunatics are locked up and treated as criminals. In the country, they are allowed to roam about as long as they are not violent. But nothing is done to help them, and no-one even tries to understand their problems."

But the Duke had tried, Leona told herself.

All the many doctors he had consulted on his son's behalf, and the many treatments the Marquess had undergone, had not been able to restore his damaged brain.

There was no understanding why such a deformation of nature had occurred, but it had! And to think of being married to such a man made Leona feel physically sick.

She was very innocent, having no idea what was involved in the begetting of a child, or how a man made love to a woman so that they became in actual fact man and wife.

She was only sure it was something close and intimate.

The thought of being touched by those hot hands with their warm skin and a hidden strength made her whole body shudder in disgust.

She knew that, while the Duke had pleaded with her and put his case logically and persuasively, he was determined that she should obey him. In fact she had little chance of escape.

He had made it quite clear that if she refused he would turn her from the Castle without a penny with which to support herself.

But would she in fact be able to escape?

Had the strange feeling that she was a prisoner, which she had had ever since coming to Ardness Castle, become a reality?

Tomorrow, however much she might protest, however desperately she might fight against it, she felt that inexorably the Duke would drag her again into the Marquess's presence.

The Minister would be there and almost before she knew what was happening they would be man and wife!

And after that?

Leona's mind shied away from the very thought of it.

The Duke's suggestion that later, when she had produced the heir he wanted, she would be free to take a lover, shocked her to the point when she thought she was being tempted into sin by the Devil himself!

"Mama! Mama!" she cried in the darkness. "What am I to do? How can I escape?"

She had the feeling that the servants would be told not to let her ride alone again with only a groom for company.

All tomorrow the Duke himself would be watching her, breaking down her resistance, refusing to listen to anything she might say to bring about any alteration to his plans.

"I cannot . . . do it! I . . . cannot!" she told herself.

She heard the Marquess's voice slurring over her

name and the cry that had come from the room after
they had left it.

At the back of her mind there was a memory of
something which had occurred many years before.

She had never thought about it again until this
moment, and yet now it was coming back to her
thoughts.

She had been quite young at the time, but she
remembered there had been some trouble over a girl
who lived in the village.

Leona could not even remember the girl's name,
but she could recall her father being very angry.

"It is a disgrace!" he had declared. "The man is
not sane—not normal! He should be shut up and
not allowed to roam free to molest decent young girls!"

"He is quite quiet, darling, except when the moon
is full," her mother answered.

"The moon! The moon!" her father ejaculated
angrily. "It is an excuse for every sexual crime in the
calendar! If it really does send these beasts roaming
after innocent girls, then they should be constrained."

"It is very unfortunate," Leona's mother murmured.

"Unfortunate?" her father shouted. "And what will
become of the wretched little bastard who will be the
result of this moon-struck monster's act of violence?"

Her mother had not answered and her father had
gone from the room, slamming the door behind him.

"What has happened? Why is Papa so angry?"
Leona had asked.

"It is nothing you would understand, darling,"
her mother replied.

"But who is this girl who has been hurt, Mama?"

"It is just one of the village girls who helps in the
garden at fruit-picking time," her mother replied.

Then she sighed.

"Poor child. I must go and see her and do what
I can to help."

Now Leona could remember the anger in her
father's voice and the way he had said:

"The moon-struck monster's act of violence."

Fearfully her eyes went towards the window and she saw as she expected a silver light on either side of the curtains!

It was all a tangled toil that she could not unravel, but the horror of it so pervaded her mind that she could only lie tense, knowing that inexorably tomorrow would come and she would have to face what was waiting for her.

Suddenly she heard a sound.

It was something she had listened for night after night but never heard.

Now it was there!

Someone was coming down the corridor with slow, stealthy footsteps.

She tried to tell herself it must be Mrs. McKenzie, but she knew the tread was too heavy for it to be a woman.

She sat up in bed, her heart beating wildly, and remembered with relief that after the maids had left her she had locked the door.

This was something she had never done since she had stayed at Ardness Castle.

But tonight she had thought she was going to cry, to burst into bitter weeping because she had lost the man she loved, and she did not wish anyone to see her humiliation and despair.

Several times since she had come to the Castle Mrs. McKenzie had returned to her room after she was in bed, to bring her a warm drink or to make up the fire.

She knew it was only a respectful attention on the Housekeeper's part.

Although once she had been nearly asleep and disliked being disturbed, she had managed to thank Mrs. McKenzie politely.

But tonight she could not bear to answer the questions Mrs. McKenzie might ask if she came in and found her crying. So she had locked the door and it was reassuring to know that whoever was outside could not get in.

But it was far too late, Leona realised, for it to be Mrs. McKenzie or one of the housemaids.

The footsteps stopped outside her door.

She was very still in the big bed and although she could not see the handle of the door she knew it was turning.

There was just the faint sound of it.

Then outside there was the deep and heavy breathing of a man who, she told herself, was excited at the thought of what he was about to do.

She knew then that it was the Marquess who was seeking her, and she pressed her hand hastily over her mouth to still the scream of fear that rose in her throat.

The handle turned again and now there was nothing surreptitious about it. Rattling loudly, it turned right and left.

Then there was a heavy bang as if someone had put a shoulder to the door, but it was strong and some part of her mind told her it would not be possible for anyone to break in easily.

At the same time, she was terrified to the point where her lips were dry and her forehead was wet.

The breathing grew more intense.

"Leona!—Pretty—Leona!"

Leona pressed her hand even tighter over her mouth.

The Marquess spoke again.

"My—wife—Leona! I—want—you! I—want—you!"

It was impossible to move, impossible to breathe.

Then when she felt she must suffocate from holding her breath, Leona heard the footsteps moving away.

Slowly the sound of them retreated into the distance.

She listened and listened until she thought she heard a door slam.

Only then did she collapse against the pillows, trembling violently in her horror of what might have happened.

Then suddenly a question arose in her mind that would not be denied.

Had the Duke deliberately planned that the Marquess should come to her room tonight and force her into a position where she would be obliged to marry him, whatever her feelings in the matter?

It was an idea that she could hardly credit, and it seemed extraordinary that all the time she had been at Ardness Castle she had not even been aware that the Marquess was there.

Yet tonight, at a moment when what he had intended to do would prove a far more forcible argument than anything the Duke might say, he had escaped from the doctor who looked after him and had come from the secrecy of his own rooms to find her.

He had been excited by seeing her, excited too by the moon outside, and tomorrow this monster—this lunatic—would be her husband!

Frantically, in a panic that swept everything from Leona's mind but a determination to escape, she jumped out of bed and started to dress.

There was no need to light a candle, she had only to pull back the curtains to let in the moonlight.

It flooded in, gloriously silver, illuminating the whole room.

A full moon, beautiful in itself, yet, Leona knew, instrumental in driving that creature who was not really a man to the point when he desired her physically—as his wife!

Chapter Six

The heather was deep and Leona had to struggle through it.

She felt, as she climbed up the hill, that it was trying to prevent her escape, pulling at her, catching at her gown, impeding her progress, so that every moment the panic within her seemed to be rising.

Frequently she looked back over her shoulder and saw by the light of the moon that the Castle looked more grim and frightening than ever.

The darkness of the valley behind it was menacing and every moment she expected to hear shouts and to find that she was being pursued.

Her gown was caught by a bramble, and as she wrenched it away she heard its thin material tear.

She had been so frantic to escape that she had put on the first gown on which her hand rested in the wardrobe.

She realised now that it was not one of the new, elaborate frocks that the Duke had given her, but one she had made herself of pink batiste which was most unsuitable for walking over the moors.

At the same time, although the skirt was full, she was not encumbered by a whale-bone crinoline, which would have impeded her further.

She had snatched a woollen shawl from a drawer, and without arranging her hair, which fell loose over her shoulders, she had gone to her bed-room door to stand holding her breath and listening.

113

How could she be sure that the Marquess was not still outside in the corridor, perhaps waiting until she should appear?

But there was no sound to be heard, and after a few minutes, very, very cautiously and slowly Leona unlocked her bed-room door and peeped outside.

The corridor was almost in darkness save for two or three sconces in which the candles had not been extinguished.

They gave enough light for her to see that there was no-one there to watch her creep on tip-toe towards the main part of the Castle.

She was well aware that it would be foolish to try to leave by the front door, even if she were able to turn the massive lock or pull back the heavy bolts.

But there was, she knew, a door which opened on to the garden, and here she found that the lock was not beyond her strength.

She let herself out, felt the night air on her face, then ran as fast as she could across the lawns to find cover in the bushes of rhododendrons which bordered them.

She made her way through a wild shrubbery beyond the cultivated gardens, and then by climbing over the fence she was on the moor itself.

She had moved so quickly that already she was breathless, and the climb up the steep sides of the hill through the thick heather was progressively exhausting.

Driven by panic, she struggled on, feeling that if she was captured now and taken back to the Castle there would be no hope of ever escaping again.

Up up, up she climbed, making no effort to find the sheep-tracks which would have made her ascent easier, but just taking a direct and exhaustingly steep route up towards the cairn.

It was impossible to think of anything except getting away. She did not even remember for the moment that Lord Strathcairn had betrayed her love.

All she knew was that she must be off the Duke's land before he discovered she was not in the Castle.

Finally, when her heart was beating so violently with the exertion that she felt it must burst from her breast and her breath was coming in short gasps, she reached the top of the hill.

Now she could see that the cairn was a little way to her right.

As she looked at it she caught her foot and fell forward, fighting for breath and clutching at tufts of heather as if they were a lifeline that would save her from drowning.

For a few minutes it was impossible to breathe, impossible to go further, until with a supernatural effort she forced herself to her feet and struggled on.

She knew now where she was going.

There was only one sanctuary where she would find safety.

She hurried down from the summit, and before she reached it she could hear the sound of the cascade falling onto the rocks beneath it and see the water shimmer silver in the moonlight.

"I am safe!" Leona told herself. "I am safe!"

She stood for a moment looking down at the cascade, knowing that once she was behind the veil of water she would be safely concealed in the cave that had hidden the Chieftains of the McCairns after Culloden.

She remembered that few people knew of its existence.

'I am safe!' she thought again. 'Thank you, God.'

She raised her face to the stars, realising now that there was no hurry and some hours must pass before dawn.

Then feeling suddenly very tired she moved down to the rushing water.

Without much difficulty she found the place where Lord Strathcairn had pulled aside the heather to show her the narrow passage along which she could move behind the cascade.

It was very dark in the cavern, but she was no longer afraid, and moved forward confidently into the darkness to sink down onto the floor against a boulder which supported her back.

She stretched out her legs in front of her and saw that her stockings were torn to pieces and there were tears in the hem of her gown.

But it was of no consequence, just as it did not matter that her legs were scratched and bleeding. Although she had not even felt the roughness of the twigs and the thistles through which she had walked, her legs were now beginning to smart.

"I have escaped! I have escaped!" Leona whispered.

But then she remembered again the horror that she had felt when the Marquess tried to get into her room, and she trembled at the thought of him.

"I have to . . . plan what I shall . . . do now," she told herself, but found it difficult to think coherently.

Forcing her brain to work, she decided that when it was day-break she would start walking towards Cairn Castle.

She was sure that the stalkers who were watching on Lord Strathcairn's instructions would tell him of her arrival.

'I shall ask him to lend me money with which to return home,' she thought. 'At least if the house is not yet sold, I can stay there until I find some work to do.'

If in fact the farmer had found a purchaser, then she would have enough money to keep her from starvation.

'There is no-one else I can . . . ask except . . . Lord Strathcairn,' she thought helplessly.

She knew it would be an agony to see him again and a humiliation that she must accept his assistance, but there was no alternative.

At the same time, even to think of him was to feel an agonising pain within her heart because he had deceived her.

She knew now that he was everything she had longed for and hoped to find in a man.

The sense of protection he had given her when he had held her in his arms had awakened her love even before he kissed her.

Never again in her life, she thought despairingly,

would she be able to feel for a man that same inexpressible rapture and wonder.

She felt the tears gather in her eyes at the thought of what she had lost.

Then she told herself severely that this was not the time to weep over her lost love; rather, she must make sure of being able to return to her own home in England.

The thought of going back to the emptiness and the loneliness without her mother was so poignant that Leona put her hands up to her eyes.

"Help me . . . Mama . . . help me!" she prayed.

But her prayer seemed to be lost in the sound of the cascading water and all she could remember was Lord Strathcairn's head silhouetted against it when he had taken her in his arms and his lips had found hers.

Because she was so unhappy, so desolate, and still so afraid, she allowed herself for a moment to remember the wonder of his kiss and the ecstasy he had evoked in her.

It had been something so exquisite and so spiritual that even now she could hardly credit that he had in fact been acting a lie in letting her believe that he was free to express his love.

"Oh, Torquil, how could you?" she murmured, then resolutely fought against the tears which threatened to overwhelm her.

Because she was so exhausted by her ordeal in the Castle and by her panic-stricken climb up the side of the hill, Leona sank lower on the floor of the cave.

Finally she lay down on the sand and with her hands beneath her cheek she fell asleep.

* * *

"My darling, what has happened? Why are you here?" Leona heard a voice say.

Unbelievably, Lord Strathcairn was beside her and was pulling her into his arms.

For a second she was only conscious of a wild, irresistible joy because he was there and was touching her.

"I could not believe it when I was awakened at dawn, when one of my keepers who had been up all night trying to shoot a fox reported that he had seen you cross the boundary!" Lord Strathcairn said in his deep voice.

With an effort Leona thrust aside her happiness and the sense of security he always gave her and tried to move from his encircling arms.

"I . . . I was . . . h-hiding," she stammered.

"But why? And from whom?" Lord Strathcairn asked.

He looked down at her feet and saw her torn stockings and the congealed blood on her legs.

"You are hurt!"

"I had to . . . get away, and this was the only place I could . . . come to."

He pulled her a little closer to him as he said quietly:

"Tell me what happened."

She turned her face against his shoulder, struggling for words, fighting for self-control as the terror of the night swept over her.

"The . . . Duke wants me to . . . marry his . . . son!" she whispered. "But he is . . . he is not . . . normal . . . he is . . . an . . . idiot!"

"My God!"

Lord Strathcairn held her so tightly that she could hardly breathe.

"Is that really the truth?" he asked after a moment. "Could the Duke really conceive such a plan?"

"I . . . saw the Marquess, then . . . then he tried to . . . enter my room."

She felt that Lord Strathcairn was stunned into silence and went on quickly:

"But the door was . . . locked and when he had . . . gone away I . . . came here."

"Thank God you did that!" Lord Strathcairn ejaculated. "I will take you home with me, my precious. Come, you are cold."

He pulled Leona's shawl round her protectively

and for the first time she realised that it was both chill and damp in the cavern.

She had, however, been too preoccupied to notice it before, and only now when the first daylight was percolating through the cascade could she see that the sides of the cave were streaked with damp.

Lord Strathcairn drew her to her feet.

"When we get to the Castle," he said, "you must have a hot bath and something warm to drink. Then you need no longer think of what you have left behind."

There was something so caressing and comforting in his voice that Leona weakly let it beguile her.

Although she thought she ought to tell him that she knew about his wife, she could not bring the words to her lips.

He went ahead of her to draw back the heather and she emerged to find that the pale rays of sunshine just rising in the east were sweeping away the last remnants of the night.

It glinted in Leona's eyes, making her feel that she was dazzled by the fresh loveliness of the morning.

Lord Strathcairn let the heather fall back into place, then putting his arm round her shoulders he drew her forward to where she knew his horse would be waiting.

Then as they took a few steps round the hillock they both stopped simultaneously and Leona gave a little gasp of fright.

Standing by Lord Strathcairn's horse were five men, tall, bearded, and all wearing the MacArdn tartan.

She knew without being told that they were the Duke's men who had been sent in search of her.

Even if no-one had seen her climbing the hill, she thought, the Duke would have guessed she would go over the boundary onto the Strathcairn land.

When her pursuers reached the cairn they would have seen the riderless horse.

As if to reassure her, Lord Strathcairn's arm tightened as he asked:

"What do you want?"

"His Grace instructed us, M'Lord, t' find th' lady an' bring her back to th' Castle."

"I am taking Miss Grenville home with me," Lord Strathcairn replied.

"We've had our orders, M'Lord."

There was an uncomfortable silence and Leona was aware that Lord Strathcairn was speculating what chance he had of opposing five determined men.

Before he could speak there was a sound behind them and Leona glanced round to see yet another man appear over the boundary. He was leading one of the Ardness ponies which were used by the sportsmen on the Duke's moor.

It carried a side-saddle and she realised that the Duke had been quite confident his men would find her and take her back.

She had a sudden fear that Lord Strathcairn might do something rash, and hastily before he could speak she said in a whisper:

"I must go . . . with them."

"I think we have no alternative," he said quietly, "but we will go together."

He saw the relief in her eyes. As the horse reached them he lifted her in his arms and set her on the saddle.

"Try not to be afraid," he said. "I will look after you."

Leona's heart gave a leap of gladness. Then she remembered it would be impossible for him really to protect her, since he could not offer her marriage.

He might oppose the Duke's plans, he might try to argue that she should not be forced into doing anything against her will; but, she thought miserably, the Duke had the upper hand.

"He is to all intents and purposes my guardian," she told herself, "and Torquil is only an outsider, a man who can have no claims on me whatsoever."

And yet somehow, some irrepressible instinct within her told her she could trust him.

In fact, because of her love, it was impossible to think anything else.

Whatever he had done, whatever had happened in the past, she loved him so that everything else sank into insignificance.

The keeper leading the horse Leona was riding moved ahead; Lord Strathcairn followed behind her on his animal and the five Clansmen walked behind them.

Leona wondered as they started the long descent back to the Castle whether the Duke was watching from one of the windows, triumphant that he had succeeded in bringing her back, certain that she would find it difficult to defy him again.

It took them some time to descend the hill that Leona had climbed so quickly the night before.

Even the hill-pony slipped occasionally on the loose stones, and despite the fact that she was being led back like a prisoner-of-war, Leona was glad of the keeper's restraining hand on the bridle.

On reaching the bottom of the Glen they did not go through the garden as Leona had done, but instead took the road which led up the drive so that finally they arrived at the great iron-hinged front door.

It was open and the Major Domo stood waiting in the entrance and there were a number of other servants behind him.

He glanced at Lord Strathcairn as if in surprise, then without a word led the way through the Hall and and up the wide staircase.

Now that it was possible to walk side by side, Lord Strathcairn took Leona's hand in his and held it tightly.

Her fingers were very cold and he felt them tremble.

"It is all right, my darling," he said in a low voice that only she could hear, "do not be afraid. You know that I will protect you."

She wanted to answer him, but her voice seemed to have died in her throat and her lips were dry.

She was suddenly conscious of how strange she must look in her thin, pink gown, which her mother had once said made her look like a rose-bud, with her fair hair falling loose over her shoulders and her eyes very large and frightened in her pale face.

The Major Domo reached the top of the stairs ahead of them and opened the door of the Duke's Room.

"Miss Grenville, Your Grace and Lord Strathcairn!"

His voice seemed to ring out.

The Duke was standing waiting for them on the hearth-rug, looking, Leona thought, even more autocratic and more awe-inspiring than usual.

One glance at his face was enough to tell her that he was extremely angry. There was a frown between his eyes and beneath his thick grey eye-brows his eyes seemed to glitter ominously.

He looked at Leona, then at Lord Strathcairn.

"I did not invite you here, Strathcairn," he said after a moment's pause.

"You are well aware why I have come," Lord Strathcairn replied.

"I am aware of nothing!" the Duke answered. "As I have told you before, what happens in my County, on my land, and in my Castle is none of your business!"

"I have made it my business," Lord Strathcairn replied. "As I wish to speak amicably to Your Grace on this occasion, I suggest that our disagreements of yesterday are not brought into the matter which concerns us both at this moment."

"I told you when you last spoke to me," the Duke said, "that we had nothing more to say to each other, and that as far as I was concerned you and your Clan, which has little importance beside mine, have ceased to exist. I see no reason to change my mind."

"There is every reason, Your Grace," Lord Strathcairn corrected. "But what concerns us at the moment is Leona Grenville."

"She is no concern of yours!" the Duke said sharply.

"That is untrue," Lord Strathcairn replied, "and because, as I have already said, nothing is to be gained by a violent disagreement and it might in fact disturb Leona, I wish to put my suggestions to you quietly and without anger."

He paused to ask in a conversational tone:

"May I sit down?"

"No!" the Duke ejaculated harshly. "You have come here without my permission. I will not offer you my hospitality, and if you do not leave when I request you to do so, I will have you forcibly removed by my servants!"

Leona trembled at the violence in the Duke's voice.

Lord Strathcairn, feeling her agitation, took his arm from her and walked nearer to the Duke.

"I am trying to talk to Your Grace in a sensible, reasonable way," he said. "Will you hear what I have to say? Let Leona express her point of view, then perhaps you will begin to understand that what you are contemplating is completely and absolutely impossible!"

"How dare you challenge my authority!" the Duke stormed.

He glared at Lord Strathcairn as he spoke.

As the two men faced each other defiantly Leona heard a movement just behind her.

She thought it must be a servant and turned her head. Then, seeing who was approaching her, she gave a little cry and instinctively flung out her hand towards Lord Strathcairn.

But she was too late!

It was the Marquess who had come into the room, moving in a surreptitious way which had not attracted attention until he had reached Leona's side.

"Leona—pretty—Leona," he said.

He picked her up in his arms and, as she screamed, carried her away.

Both Lord Strathcairn and the Duke started forward, but the Marquess ran out of the room.

She screamed again as he rushed down the corridor with her in his arms, his feet thumping noisily as he moved with an ungainly gait, but at the same time incredibly swiftly.

Passing the top of the stairs, he ran down the corridor on the other side of it, holding Leona so tightly that she could scarcely breathe, let alone scream.

She tried to struggle but his arms were like bands of steel and she knew there was an almost diabolical strength in his madness.

They reached the end of the corridor and now she could hear voices behind them and the sound of men running.

The Marquess pulled open the door of the tower and she had a glimpse of the stone stairs leading upwards before he pulled her even closer against him and her face was buried in his coat.

Up the stairs he pounded and again she tried to struggle, but to no avail.

They reached the landing at the top.

There the Marquess paused for a moment to drag down from the wall a claymore which rested beneath a shield.

The Duke had told Leona when she first visited the tower that they were the weapons kept by the ancient guards who watched for their enemies.

The Marquess dragged Leona through the door onto the roof of the tower and slammed it behind him.

"Let me . . . go!" she began to say frantically, then realised that it was not the way to deal with a lunatic.

She looked up into the Marquess's face.

She could see by the glitter in his eyes and the saliva on his wet lips that he was in the grip of some insane frenzy.

"Put me down . . . Euan," she said gently.

"Leona—mine!" he said fiercely. "My—wife—I—want—you!"

"You are hurting me," Leona said, "and that is unkind."

The quietness in her voice seemed to have some effect upon him.

"Pretty—Leona," he said. "Pretty—pretty—Leona."

But there was still a wild look in his eyes which was terrifying.

"Please put me down," Leona pleaded. "I want to tidy my hair so that it will look pretty."

He was so strong and so large that she realised he could hold her completely immobile with one arm and she could not move.

In his other hand he held the claymore.

Slowly, reluctantly, he let her feet touch the ground.

With a superhuman effort Leona forced herself to smile at him.

"Thank you," she said. "You are kind, Euan."

"Kind—to—Leona," he said slowly. "My—wife—mine!"

She tried to move a little way away from him, frightened that if she did anything hastily he would clutch at her again.

Then as he stood looking at her and she felt there was something in his scrutiny and his shining eyes to which she dare not put a name, the door from the tower burst open behind them.

It was the Duke who stood there.

"Come here at once, Euan!" he commanded. "Do you hear me? Come here!"

The Marquess turned his head and Leona thought with a sensation of relief that he was going to obey the Duke.

Then he stepped forward and with a sudden thrust drove the claymore into his father's chest!

The Duke did not cry out, but his mouth opened

almost ludicrously as the force of the blow sent him reeling backwards. Then there was the sound of his body rolling down the stairs.

The Marquess laughed and shut the tower door again.

For a moment Leona could hardly believe what she had seen.

The horror of the claymore entering the Duke's chest, the blood she could now see on the blade, and the manner in which the old man had fallen down the stairs were all too incredible for her to believe it had actually occurred.

Then as she put both hands up to her cheeks, staring at the Marquess with terrified eyes, he pushed into place a heavy iron bolt at the top of the door.

"Alone—with—pretty—Leona," he said happily.

Now there was a look in his eyes that frightened her more than any expression she had seen on his face before.

She tried to think coherently, but it was impossible.

She looked at the sword and the Duke's blood on the tip of the blade and felt she must faint.

"Throw away the sword, Euan . . . throw it . . . away!" she pleaded. "It is . . . ugly! Throw it away!"

He seemed to understand what she was saying, for after a moment he replied:

"Ugly—too—ugly—for—pretty—Leona."

"Yes, that is right," Leona answered. "Ugly!"

It seemed that he wished to please her, for he walked across the roof to stand looking over the battlements down into the courtyard below.

Leona had not moved but now she heard voices and she recognised one as being that of Dr. Bronson.

"Come down, My Lord! I want to talk to you!" Dr. Bronson shouted. "It is time for your breakfast. Come to me, and we will have it together."

The Marquess was still looking down and now Leona moved to the battlements.

Below, a long way down, because the tower was high, she could see Dr. Bronson and with him were a number of servants, including the Major Domo.

She had hoped to see Lord Strathcairn, but he was not there.

"Come down, My Lord! You know what you are doing is wrong. Come down!"

Again Dr. Bronson was reasoning with his patient, and Leona glanced at the Marquess to see if there was any response.

She saw that there was an almost mischievous smile on his thick lips, as leaning over the battlements he threw the claymore directly at the doctor!

Dr. Bronson moved just in time and the sword missed him by a hair's breadth. As he jumped out of the way the Marquess laughed the loud, unrestrained laugh of an idiot.

"Dead! All—dead!" he said happily, and moved towards Leona.

She tried to escape him but he caught her easily.

Now once again he held her suffocatingly close, his arms entwined about her, and it was impossible to move.

"Leona—pretty—Leona!" he said in a thick voice. "Mine! Mine!"

She anticipated what he was about to do and buried her face in his shoulder.

But she could feel his mouth against her hair and the horror of it made her feel as if she must die from the terror which seemed to strike at her as effectively as any claymore.

"Leona—pretty—Leona!" the Marquess was saying again.

Now there was a rising excitement in his voice that was unmistakable and Leona felt as if the bear-like grip with which he enfolded her might break her ribs.

He was nuzzling her hair and because even his chin had a strength that was irresistible, he was pushing her head back from his shoulder and she felt his lips on her forehead.

She screamed and as she did so she heard a voice behind them say:

"Stop! Stop that immediately!"

The voice was so commanding that the Marquess loosened his grip as he turned his head, and Leona could see Lord Strathcairn climbing over the battlement.

She realised that he must in fact have climbed up the outside of the tower.

She was aware of the danger and that he had risked his life even as he stepped safely onto the roof to walk towards them.

She felt the Marquess tense his muscles.

She knew that he was about to spring on Lord Strathcairn, perhaps to hurl him, as he had hurled the claymore, from the top of the tower.

"Be careful! Be careful!" she screamed.

As if he too realised the danger, Lord Strathcairn pulled the skean-dhu from the top of his stocking and, taking the dagger in his right hand, moved forward with the blade pointing at the Marquess.

"Let her go!" he said commandingly, and astonishingly the Marquess obeyed.

Leona felt him take his arms from her. Then she saw that he was gazing at the naked blade of the skean-dhu with something like terror in his eyes.

"No—more—hurt," he said with a sudden change in the tone of his voice. "Not—hurt—too—much—pain! Go—away!"

Still pointing the blade at him, Lord Strathcairn moved slowly nearer and nearer until with a convulsive movement Leona could reach out and take his free hand.

As she did so, the Marquess backed even further away, his eyes still held as if mesmerised by the sharp blade of the dagger glinting in the sunshine.

He retreated step by step.

Then just as Lord Strathcairn realised what was happening and lowered the point of the skean-dhu, the Marquess reached the side of the tower.

He was bending backwards, and he was standing at a place where the crenellation was low.

His feet may have slipped or perhaps it was his

huge ungainly body that unbalanced him, but whatever the reason, as Leona watched, paralysed with horror, he fell backwards.

His arms shot out and for a moment he seemed to be suspended like a great bird of prey against the sky. Then he vanished from sight.

It was impossible to scream, impossible to breathe . . . she only knew that the world had gone . . . dark. . . .

* * *

Leona came back to consciousness to find herself being carried by arms which gave her a sense of security and an inescapable happiness.

For a moment she could remember nothing except that she was where she wanted to be.

Then as they reached the last step of the tower she could see the walls of the corridor and hear the voices and footsteps hurrying up the stairs.

"Brandy!" Lord Strathcairn ordered sharply above her head.

Holding her against his chest, he carried her into the Duke's Room and set her down gently on the sofa.

He would have taken his arms from her but she clung to him.

"It is all right, my darling," he said. "It is all over now."

She murmured something incoherent and he went down on his knees beside the sofa to hold her against him so that she could hide her face.

With his free hand he swept back her hair.

"You are safe," he reassured her.

The servants must have brought the brandy he ordered, for now he held a glass to her lips.

"Drink it, my darling," he said.

As she did so she remembered how the Duke had given her brandy the night before.

She felt the fiery spirit reviving her and asked hesitatingly:

"Is the . . . Duke . . . dead?"

Lord Strathcairn must have looked enquiringly

at the Major Domo, who stood beside them as he answered:

"I'm afraid so, M'Lord. 'Twas not only th' wound in his chest, but His Grace also fell a long way down th' stone stairs."

Leona tried to repress a feeling of relief.

She could still see the almost ludicrous expression of astonishment on the old man's face when his son struck at him. She wondered if ever again life could be normal and ordinary after such terrible things had occurred.

As if he understood what she was feeling, Lord Strathcairn said:

"Do you feel well enough for me to take you away from here? I have the idea you do not wish to stay."

"P-please . . . take me . . . please!" Leona begged.

He rose from the side of the sofa.

"I am taking Miss Grenville back to Cairn Castle," he said to the Major Domo. "I shall ride over the moor because it is quicker. Have everything she possesses packed and sent immediately by road."

"That'll be done, M'Lord."

There was no mistaking the respectful note in the Major Domo's voice.

Lord Strathcairn bent down and picking Leona up in his arms he carried her down the stairs into the big Entrance-Hall.

She shut her eyes not only because she wished never to see Ardness Castle again, but also for fear of what else she might see.

Perhaps the dead body of the Duke or perhaps that of his son.

Without speaking, Lord Strathcairn set her on his horse that was waiting outside the front door and sprang up behind her as he had done the first day they met.

They moved off, the Major Domo and the servants watching them leave in silence. Then after they had proceeded down the drive Lord Strathcairn turned towards the moors.

It was only when Leona felt that the shadow of

the Castle was no longer over them that she raised her head a little to look up at him.

She could see the squareness of his chin and she thought, as she had before, that there was a faint smile on his lips.

They were moving slowly up the sharp incline and when they had nearly reached the top Leona asked:

"How could you have . . . climbed the tower?"

"I told you that I would protect you, even if it meant climbing into the sky or down into the bowels of the earth."

"You . . . might have . . . killed yourself."

"But I am safe and so, my darling one, are you."

There was silence until Leona said in a very small voice:

"I was . . . coming to the Castle this morning to ask you to . . . lend me enough money so that I . . . could go . . . home."

"Is that what you wish to do?"

"There is . . . nothing else I . . . can do!"

"I thought we might be married this evening."

He felt her stiffen in his arms, then she said hardly above a whisper:

"The Duke . . . told me you had a . . . wife!"

For a moment Lord Strathcairn did not reply. Then he asked:

"You believed him?"

"He . . . said you were . . . married to an . . . actress."

"I thought you loved me."

"I do!" Leona answered before she could stop herself. "I love you but . . ."

Her voice died away.

"But you were prepared to credit that I would say what I did to you, that I would hold you in my arms and kiss you, when I had no right to do so?"

She drew her breath.

Something glorious and wonderful was sweeping away the frozen misery that had encompassed her heart.

"It is . . . not true?" she questioned, her eyes raised to his.

"I believed you trusted me."

"I wanted to . . . I longed to . . . but . . . but you never asked me to . . . marry you."

"I thought you understood that there was no other possibility in the world for either of us."

"Then . . . what the Duke said was . . . a lie!"

"A lie, my darling," Lord Strathcairn replied, "but like many falsehoods it had a slight foundation of truth about it, which I presume makes it excusable in the circumstances."

"I thought it was . . . true."

"I would have told you, if it had even crossed my mind that the past would rise to disturb you."

He paused to look down at her.

"It did disturb you?"

Her eyes looked into his beseechingly.

"I thought . . . everything in which I had . . . believed had been . . . smashed and . . . shattered," she murmured.

"I should have felt the same," Lord Strathcairn said.

"I wanted to . . . believe in your . . . love," Leona said, "but the Duke was so . . . positive and I thought perhaps as you had not asked me to . . . marry you . . . it was because you . . . could not do so."

"From the moment I saw you," Lord Strathcairn replied, "I knew that you belonged to me and that I had been waiting for you. I would have told you that very first night when we dined together what you meant to me, but I was afraid."

"Afraid?" Leona questioned.

He drew a deep breath.

They had reached the top of the hill and now he pulled his horse to a standstill beside the cairn and looked out over the moors ahead of them to where the Loch lay golden in the sunshine, Cairn Castle rising above it.

"When I was very young and still at Oxford," he

said quietly, "I fell in love, not with a play-actress, but with a concert-singer who had a very beautiful voice.

"She was older than I was, but I believed she loved me. She told me she did and I brought her home to the Castle."

Leona felt a pang of jealousy but she waited, her eyes on Lord Strathcairn's face as he went on:

"I told my family and everyone that we were engaged and Isobel seemed delighted with my home and my people."

His lips tightened and Leona thought there was a note of cynicism in his voice as he continued:

"I was very young and very gullible. I found that while Isobel might have married me, she found the gaiety and amusement of the south irresistible.

"She had no intention of settling down in an obscure Scottish Castle with no audience except her husband."

Leona made a little movement, but she did not speak. She felt there was nothing she could say.

"I took her back to the world to which she belonged," Lord Strathcairn went on. "But because I was young and proud I did not admit to anyone, not even to my father, that the engagement was broken off."

He looked down at Leona and smiled.

"It now seems ridiculous and foolish that my pride could have hurt you, my precious one."

"But why did the Duke think you were married?" Leona asked.

"I think a great many people thought that," Lord Strathcairn replied. "They imagined that I had married Isobel in the south but that her profession prevented her from coming north. Because I would not admit the truth, I never denied the rumours that we were man and wife."

He gave a little laugh.

"Perhaps I felt at the time that they protected me from being pursued as a bachelor. Whatever it was, I let the gossips have their way; and now I am punished by knowing that entirely through such stupidity I hurt you."

"I meant . . . never to . . . see you . . . again," Leona whispered.

"Do you think I would have allowed you to escape me?" Lord Strathcairn enquired. "I was coming to Ardness Castle today to tell the Duke I intended to marry you and, if he refused, to ask you to run away with me."

"You know I would have done so," Leona said, her eyes shining.

Then she added a little doubtfully:

"If it had been possible! I have a feeling the Duke would have prevented it somehow."

"That is something he cannot do now," Lord Strathcairn said. "We will be married this evening, and then nothing and no-one can ever come between us."

"You are quite certain you . . . want me?" Leona asked.

He looked into her eyes and she felt a little quiver go through her because of the fire in his.

Then his lips were on hers and she knew that once again he was arousing in her the ecstasy and the wonder she had felt when he first kissed her in the cave.

Chapter Seven

Leona vaguely heard people moving in the room and felt as if she came back to consciousness through layers and layers of soft cloud.

Then with a start she realised she was at Cairn Castle.

She was safe and she was to marry Lord Strathcairn!

The knowledge flooded over her like sunshine and she opened her eyes to see Mrs. McCray and the maids bringing in the bath to set it down in front of the fire.

It seemed as if centuries of time had passed since the morning, when they had arrived at the Castle.

Only as Lord Strathcairn had lifted her down from the horse's back did she realise how tired she was.

The fact that she had slept only for a short time the night before, the terror that had driven her to the cavern behind the cascade, and the horror she had experienced when the Marquess carried her to the top of the tower had left her physically depleted.

At the same time, in her exhaustion her brain kept questioning if the horror was really over and she need no longer be afraid.

As if he understood what she was feeling, Lord Strathcairn had swept her up into his arms and carried her up the staircase, as he had done the first time she had come to the Castle.

"I want you to go to sleep, my darling," he said gently. "I want you to remember nothing, to think of nothing, except that I love you!"

He carried her into a bed-room and Mrs. McCray and Maggy had come running to help her undress.

Almost before Leona's head was on the pillow she was asleep.

Now she knew she must have slept away all the hours of the day and, though she felt refreshed, she regretted that she had wasted so much time in sleeping when she might have been with Lord Strathcairn.

Then she remembered!

He had said they were to be married that evening and at the thought of it she sat up quickly in bed.

"Ye're awake, Miss," Mrs. McCray said in the warm tone that Leona remembered so well. "Your gowns have arrived an' we've unpacked them. Maggy and Janet will bring them in when ye've bathed."

Maggy left the room and Mrs. McCray came nearer to the bed to say:

"I've a message from the Laird for ye, Miss."

"What is it?" Leona asked.

"The Laird says that if ye dinna wish to be married in yon gowns ye've brought with ye from Ardness, I was tae suggest that ye might wish tae see the wedding-gowns that are kept here in the Castle."

"Wedding-gowns?" Leona exclaimed.

"Aye, Miss," Mrs. McCray replied. "It's been the tradition for many generations that the wedding-gown o' every Chieftain's wife should be preserved. There are a number of them kept in a special room where I care for them and see they're not damaged by the moths."

Leona was still for a moment.

She knew, now that she thought of it, that she could not bear to marry Lord Strathcairn in a gown that had been paid for by the Duke.

It would be foolish, she thought, to refuse to wear

them on other occasions, but a wedding-gown was different, something sacred.

"Thank you, Mrs. McCray. I would like to see them . . . but how could the Laird have . . . known that was how I would . . . feel?" she added almost beneath her breath.

Mrs. McCray smiled.

"Ye must have realised by now that the Laird is fey?"

"He is?" Leona exclaimed.

"Ever since he was a wee bairn, the Laird has known what other people are thinking and feeling. And he has moments when the Vision burns in him and he sees the future."

"My mother told me that many Scots have 'Second Sight.' "

"Och, aye," Mrs. McCray agreed. "That's true. And now, Miss, shall I bring some o' the gowns for ye to see?"

"That would be very kind."

Later, when Leona was dressed in a gown which she learnt had belonged to Lord Strathcairn's grandmother, she thought that nothing could become her better.

Married in 1785, the future Lady Strathcairn had chosen a gown which was not unlike those that were in fashion at the moment, except that it had no crinoline.

The skirt was full and the tight bodice was softly draped with lace which blended with the exquisite lace veil, centuries old, which Mrs. McCray carried almost reverently in her arms.

When it had been draped over Leona's golden head it was surmounted by a tiara of diamonds set in the shape of thistles which had been worn by every Chieftain's wife for centuries.

With her fair hair and blue eyes Leona knew that she looked almost unreal and she only hoped that Lord Strathcairn would think once again that she resembled the mists rising over the Loch.

Her bouquet was of white roses from the garden, and she remembered that Lord Strathcairn had said that she resembled a white rose in bud.

"Make him always think me so pure and perfect," she prayed.

She felt very shy when she went from her bed-room down the passage to the room where he was waiting for her.

She loved him. She loved him so overwhelmingly that she could hardly believe it was true that she was to be his wife.

At the same time, now that the dramatic events in which they had both taken part were over, she realised that they knew little about each other, and she felt very young and inexperienced.

Lord Strathcairn was nine years older than she was, a nobleman and a Chieftain, the owner of great properties, and a leader of men.

"Suppose I . . . fail him?" she questioned herself, and her eyes were worried as she looked up into his face.

He stood staring at her and for a moment he did not speak. Then in a voice that vibrated with emotion he said:

"I have no words, my darling, in which to tell you how beautiful you are!"

She felt a little quiver run through her, then she said:

"It was . . . kind of you to think that I . . . might wear your . . . grandmother's gown!"

"I think if she knew she would be as proud of you as I am!"

"Do you . . . mean that?"

"We have many years ahead of us in which I shall tell you how much you mean to me and how very much I love you," Lord Strathcairn replied. "But now, my dearest heart, the Minister is waiting for us and I am impatient for you to be my wife."

He offered Leona his arm and she slipped her hand into it. Then he led her towards the stairs and she knew where they were to be married.

What more fitting place, she wondered, than the Chief's Room, redolent with the history of the Mc-Cairns, where the Clan had assembled in times of victory or defeat, in good times and in bad.

They walked upstairs without speaking, and Leona knew that Lord Strathcairn had deliberately not kissed her or touched her in any way.

She had known he wished to do so, she had seen the light in his eyes when he looked into hers, and she felt that his heart was beating as tumultuously as hers was.

But they both were dedicating themselves to the ceremony that lay ahead.

The door of the Chief's Room was open and now Leona could see that the walls were lined with the Clansmen, a brilliant display of colour in their kilts and sporrans.

There were no women present, only the men.

The enormous long room was decorated with heather, great bunches of it in every available space, even tucked into the shields and pikes on the walls and above the pictures.

The whole room was symbolic of Scotland.

At the far end, the Minister was waiting in his black robes, and behind him were huge bowls of white heather, so much of it that Leona felt everyone must have scoured the moors for the whole day to find it.

Moving slowly but proudly, Lord Strathcairn led her down the length of the room, until they stopped in front of the Minister, a white-haired man with a kindly face.

He opened his book and the service began.

The simple words which joined her for all time to the man she loved would be, Leona knew, engraved in her mind and heart for the rest of her life.

She felt her whole being respond to them, praying that she might make her husband happy and she might give him sons as fine as he himself was.

Then they knelt in front of the Minister and as he joined their hands Leona felt the strength of Lord

Strathcairn's fingers and knew that she would be safe
and protected as long as she lived.

The ring was on her finger and after the Minister
had blessed them they rose and quite unselfconscious-
ly Lord Strathcairn took his wife in his arms and
kissed her.

It was a gentle, dedicated kiss, and yet Leona felt
that spiritually in that moment she gave him her lips,
her heart, and her soul.

The pipes blared forth as they walked back down
the Chief's Room amid the cheers of the Clansmen
and the piper led them down the stairs and into the
Sitting-Room.

Servants closed the doors and they were alone.

For a moment they just stood looking at each
other. Then Lord Strathcairn held out his arms and
Leona moved towards him.

"My wife!" he exclaimed.

The words seemed to express his love far more
effectively than any others might have done.

"We are . . . married . . . we are . . . really married!" she whispered.

There was relief as well as exaltation in her
voice; for after all she had been through she had been
so afraid that at the last moment something might
prevent him from marrying her.

She thought she had lost him when the Duke
told her he was already married, and he might easily
have been killed when he had climbed the tower.

Her thoughts shied away from imagining what
the Marquess might have done if he had not been
afraid of the steel blade of the skean-dhu.

But that was all over.

Now there was only their future together to think
about and plan for.

Lord Strathcairn drew her to the window and
she saw that the sun was sinking in a blaze of glory
over the Loch, which was shimmering gold, and the
lights on the hills were unbelievably lovely.

"Your Kingdom, my precious!" he said. "Just as
you will always be the Queen of my heart."

"You must . . . help me to do what is . . . right and
what you . . . wish me to . . . do," Leona said in a low
voice.

"Everything about you is perfect!" he replied.
"But will what I can give you be enough?"

She knew then that at the back of his mind
there was still the hurt that had been inflicted on him
when Isobel had craved for the south and to live the
life that was not his.

In that moment Leona knew that she must con-
stantly reassure him that where she was concerned
such fears were groundless.

She raised her face to his.

"All I ask of life," she said softly, "is that I shall
be with . . . you. It does not matter whether we are
in this Castle or in some small croft tucked away under the hills. It is being . . . together which matters . . .
belonging . . . as I belong to you at this moment."

She saw the light in his eyes and the expression
on his face, which seemed to transform it.

He drew her close to him and kissed her until she
could no longer breathe or think, but only know that
she was his as he was hers.

The Butler came to tell them that dinner was
ready and they moved into the Dining-Room with its
red curtains which Leona loved.

The servants brought in food over which the
Cook had excelled himself and there was even a
hastily iced wedding-cake because, as Lord Strathcairn said with a smile, no wedding was complete
without one.

Although there was so much to talk about, there
were moments when their eyes met and there was no
need for words.

Heart was speaking to heart, spirit to spirit, man
to woman, and their happiness encircled them like an
aura of light.

It was only when the servants had withdrawn
and Lord Strathcairn sat back at his ease in his high-
backed chair with a glass of port at his side that
Leona said:

"I know we will not wish to . . . talk of it very often . . . but I cannot help . . . wondering why the Marquess was . . . born as he was."

Lord Strathcairn paused a moment before he replied:

"There may be a medical explanation, I do not know. But in Scotland I know that everyone will believe that what happened today was the result of the curse!"

"A curse!" Leona exclaimed.

"I would not have thought of telling you about it before," he answered, "because it might have upset you, but every Duke of Ardness has been cursed for the last two hundred years!"

"But why?" Leona enquired. "And by whom?"

Lord Strathcairn took a sip of port before he began:

"Some men from Ross brought their ship into harbour one night because the sea was so rough they could proceed no further. They asked permission of the Chieftain to walk across Ardness land to their own County and return when the weather was more clement."

Leona was listening wide-eyed as Lord Strathcairn continued:

"Permission was granted and the men came ashore, carrying the spoils of what had been a very successful voyage."

"How many were there?" Loena enquired.

"I imagine about fifteen or twenty," Lord Strathcairn replied, "and it was dusk as they proceeded up the Glen."

Leona felt that the Glen must have seemed as dark and menacing to them as it had to her, but she did not speak and Lord Strathcairn went on:

"The Chief and the Clansmen were greedy and they lay in wait for the men from Ross. When they reached the centre of the Glen they sprang on them!"

"That was wicked!" Leona exclaimed.

"It outraged every code of decency and hospitality," Lord Strathcairn agreed. "Then, having stripped them of everything they owned, the Mac-Ardns buried them by the road-side and went back to the Castle."

"The Rosses were all killed?" Leona asked. "There was no-one left to tell the tale?"

Lord Strathcairn shook his head.

"No-one," he answered. "Their wives, sweet-hearts, and their Chieftain waited in vain for their return."

"And the ship?" Leona enquired.

"The MacArdns appropriated it because they said it had remained too long in the harbour un-claimed."

"That was stealing!"

"It was indeed!" Lord Strathcairn agreed.

"How did anyone find out what had happened?"

"Five years passed," he replied, "before the Bard of the Rosses, a man with 'Second Sight,' told the Clan that he was continually disturbed by the voices of the missing Clansmen crying out for revenge."

"They listened to him?" Leona asked.

"They listened because he was sure not only that their kinsmen had been murdered, but also described graphically the actual place where their bodies would be found."

Leona drew in her breath.

"And they found them?" she questioned.

"Stealthily one night the Rosses, led by the Bard, stole in to Ardness to find, as he had prophesied, the skeletons hidden in the Glen."

"How terrible!" Leona exclaimed. "And that was why the MacArdns are cursed?"

"Not the Clan," Lord Strathcairn corrected, "but the Chieftain, for he must always bear responsibility for what happens to those he leads. As he had the right of life and death over his people, he was equal-ly responsible for their actions, but in this case he had behaved as criminally as they had!"

His voice appeared to ring out as he added:

"And in my opinion he deserved the retribution that fell upon him."

"What was the curse?" Leona asked.

"The Bard, standing in the Glen and looking towards the Castle, called on Heaven to witness that peaceful men who had come in friendship had brutally and shamefully been murdered."

Lord Strathcairn paused.

"He must have looked very impressive, for the Bards are usually tall men with long white hair and a resonant voice."

Leona could almost see the picture he conjured up. Then he said:

"So the Bard cursed the Chieftain of the MacArdns for all time—cursed him in a way that was a just retribution for the crime he had committed."

"What was the curse?" Leona asked.

She felt herself shiver at the thought of it because she was half aware what it would be.

"The Bard predicted then, and the words have proved true ever since, that every Chieftain of the MacArdns would die by the hand of treachery."

"And has that really happened?" Leona enquired.

"The last Duke was killed in a duel he fought with his wife's lover in Paris. The Duke before him was struck down by a servant he found stealing."

"And the Chiefs before that?"

Lord Strathcairn made a gesture with his hand.

"I cannot remember what happened to them all, but in every case the curse has fulfilled itself, and they have died by the hand of treachery."

"So that is the secret of the Glen!" Leona said. "When I drove through it for the first time I felt it was dark and menacing."

"And the curse menaced you, my precious. That is something I shall never forget or forgive," Lord Strathcairn said.

He put his hand out across the table and Leona laid her fingers in it.

"Shall I reassure you," he said, "by saying that there are no curses as far as I know laid on this Chieftain, who has this day been more blessed than any man could ever be."

"I know now you would never . . . behave treacherously."

"And yet you suspected I had done so."

"Forgive . . . me," she pleaded. "Please . . . forgive me."

He raised her hand to his lips, kissing first the softness of her palm, then her fingers one by one.

"There will never be anything to forgive between us," he said. "We understand each other. We are not two people, but one."

There was a fire in his eyes as he said the last word. Then with what Leona knew was an effort he said:

"You have had a long day, my precious one. You must rest. Such events as we have passed through take their toll not only of health and strength, but also of the mind."

He rose to his feet and drew Leona to hers.

"I will come and say good-night to you," he said in his deep voice. "But our whole lives are in front of us for me to tell you how beautiful you are and how greatly I love you!"

He was speaking, she thought, more to himself than to her, and because he wished it she went to her bed-room to find Mrs. McCray there waiting for her.

There were tears in the Housekeeper's eyes as she said:

"Och, M'Lady, there's never been a more beautiful, sweet-faced bride than yourself."

"Thank you, Mrs. McCray."

" 'Tis all we've ever wished for the Laird. Ye'll bring him happiness and he'll not be so lonely as he has been since his mother died."

"I will do my best to make him happy," Leona said, "and you too."

Mrs. McCray wiped her eyes.

"Tomorrow night there's to be dancing and everyone'll gather in the Chief's Room to pay their respects, to break the bannock o'er ye heads for peace and prosperity, and to bring ye gifts."

"Gifts?" Leona enquired.

"Which they have been hoarding against this very day."

"What sort of gifts?"

"Carvings of the stags' antlers and the bones of the cattle, feathers from the blackcock and the capercailzie for the Laird."

Mrs. McCray smiled.

"An' for ye, M'Lady, bobbin lace and fine knit, at which the wifies of the McCairns excel."

"They sound delightful!" Leona exclaimed.

"An' milk-white pearls from the river," Mrs. Mc-Cray went on, "an' amethysts hewn from beneath the mountains."

"How lovely! I shall look forward to receiving such exciting gifts!"

Mrs. McCray appeared to have much more to relate. Then, as if she remembered her instructions, she said:

"Tonight the Laird says ye're to rest and Maggy's awa' to fetch ye a warm drink so that ye'll sleep well."

"I am sure I shall do that."

Leona let Mrs. McCray assist her to undress, then she put on one of the nightgowns that had been sent from Edinburgh with her gowns, brushed her hair, and got into bed.

Mrs. McCray made up the fire, put the hot drink that Maggy had brought beside the bed, and blew out the candles.

Then she curtseyed and said with a sincerity that was unmistakable:

"God bless Your Ladyship. Ye've brought guid luck to the Castle—I'm a-sure o' that!"

With tears in her eyes she went from the room.

Leona leant back against the pillows, while the flames of the fire lit the room with a golden glow and there were no shadows to make her afraid.

The door opened and Lord Strathcairn came in.

He had changed from his evening-clothes into a silk robe, and she thought as he moved across the room that he seemed very tall and commanding, and yet she knew she could never be afraid of him.

He smiled at her and sat down on the side of the bed, taking her hand in his.

They looked at each other and Leona's eyes were very large in her small face and her hair seemed to shine in the light from the fire.

"We have been married in great haste," Lord Strathcairn said after a moment, "because, my darling, I wanted to be in the position to look after you, and also it was not right for you to stay in the Castle alone unless you were my wife."

"I stayed here . . . before."

It was difficult to think of what he was saying because the touch of his hands made her thrill in a manner she had not known before and she longed as she had never longed for anything in the world for him to kiss her.

"I knew from the moment I saw you that you were different from any other woman I had ever met," he said, "and my heart turned in my breast because you were near me."

He smiled.

"But because you were a stranger I was able to behave with some propriety, which now I would find extremely difficult to do!"

Leona waited expectantly and he went on:

"But because I love you more than life itself, because I have pledged myself not only to your service but also to protect you and care for you in sickness and in health, tonight I am going to let you rest."

He drew in his breath with a sound that was almost a sigh as he continued:

"As I said just now, we have all our lives in front of us for me to tell you of my love."

There was silence, then Leona said hesitatingly:

"B-but this is . . . our wedding-day."

"A day I shall never forget," Lord Strathcairn answered. "And we will celebrate it every year until we reach our Golden Wedding."

Again there was silence and Leona felt his fingers tighten on hers until they were painful as he said, and now his voice was hoarse:

"I thought when I first saw you that you were the most beautiful person I had ever seen. I thought when you came to me in your wedding-gown that it was impossible for any woman to be more lovely, and yet now, at this moment, I can find no words with which to describe you."

Leona felt herself vibrate to the desire in his voice.

She knew that he wanted her, she knew that he was holding himself rigidly under control not to kiss her, not to touch her.

Suddenly he released her hands and rose from the bed.

"I must say good-night, Leona," he said. "If you want me, if you are afraid or in any way perturbed, I am only in the next room. I shall hear if you call."

Leona realised for the first time that there was another door in the room besides the one that opened onto the corridor.

She had been so exhausted when she arrived, and so intent on thinking of her wedding-day when she awoke, that she had not really taken in the fact that she was not in the Thistle Chamber, where she had slept before.

She was in another, much larger and more impressive bed-chamber, with a carved stone fireplace which was impressive.

The bed and the windows were hung with rose-pink velvet curtains and the Coat-of-Arms of the Strathcairns was embellished on the coverlet.

She knew now that she was in the room that by right was that of the Chieftain's wife.

It seemed to her at that moment as if there were a special atmosphere of love, devotion, and faith in the room which was redolent with history.

Lord Strathcairn stood for a moment looking into the fire. Then he moved slowly towards the door which led into his own bed-room.

He had almost reached it when Leona said urgently:

"Torquill"

He stopped and looked towards her, waiting.

"There is . . . something I wish to . . . say to you."

He turned back towards the bed, coming nearer almost reluctantly, she thought, as if he was afraid of himself.

She leant back against the pillows, her long golden hair falling over them, her eyes very blue in the firelight as she looked up at him.

"What is it, Leona?"

"There is . . . something I want . . . to ask you."

He moved nearer, yet still standing stiff and high above her. He even looked a little awe-inspiring, but she was not afraid.

She was sure with a feeling that was fey that he was feeling what she felt.

"Could you not . . . come a little . . . closer?"

He bent towards her and now Leona put out her arms and said in a whisper:

"Will you not . . . kiss me . . . good-night?"

Just for a moment he seemed to hesitate, then Leona's arms were round his neck, pulling him down to her, drawing him closer and closer until his lips found hers.

She knew that he tried to be gentle, attempted to keep control of himself, but it was as if a dam had burst and the barriers were down.

He kissed her wildly, passionately, fiercely, kissing her lips, then her eyes, her cheeks, and the warm softness of her neck until she thrilled and vibrated with strange sensations she had never known before.

"I love you—God in Heaven, how I love you!" he murmured.

Then he was kissing her again, drawing her very heart from between her lips until she responded to his kisses with a wildness which echoed his.

"I love . . . you! I love . . . you!"

"My precious—my darling—my wife!"

It was a cry of triumph, the cry of a warrior, of a conqueror who attains all he has fought for, all he has desired.

Then as the flames died down there were only the soft whispers of love and the music of the wind blowing over the Loch, singing of the eternal glory of Scotland.

ABOUT THE AUTHOR

BARBARA CARTLAND, the celebrated romantic author, historian, playwright, lecturer, political speaker and television personality, has now written over 150 books. Miss Cartland has had a number of historical books published and several biographical ones, including that of her brother, Major Ronald Cartland, who was the first Member of Parliament to be killed in the War. This book had a Foreword by Sir Winston Churchill.

In private life, Barbara Cartland, who is a Dame of the Order of St. John of Jerusalem, has fought for better conditions and salaries for Midwives and Nurses. As President of the Royal College of Midwives (Hertfordshire Branch), she has been invested with the first Badge of Office ever given in Great Britain, which was subscribed to by the Midwives themselves. She has also championed the cause for old people and founded the first Romany Gypsy Camp in the world.

Barbara Cartland is deeply interested in Vitamin Therapy and is President of the British National Association for Health.

Barbara Cartland

The world's bestselling author of romantic fiction. Her stories are always captivating tales of intrigue, adventure and love.

☐	THE TEARS OF LOVE	2148	$1.25
☐	THE DEVIL IN LOVE	2149	$1.25
☐	THE ELUSIVE EARL	2436	$1.25
☐	THE BORED BRIDEGROOM	6381	$1.25
☐	JOURNEY TO PARADISE	6383	$1.25
☐	THE PENNILESS PEER	6387	$1.25
☐	NO DARKNESS FOR LOVE	6427	$1.25
☐	THE LITTLE ADVENTURE	6428	$1.25
☐	LESSONS IN LOVE	6431	$1.25
☐	THE DARING DECEPTION	6435	$1.25
☐	CASTLE OF FEAR	8103	$1.25
☐	THE GLITTERING LIGHTS	8104	$1.25
☐	A SWORD TO THE HEART	8105	$1.25
☐	THE MAGNIFICENT MARRIAGE	8166	$1.25
☐	THE RUTHLESS RAKE	8240	$1.25
☐	THE DANGEROUS DANDY	8280	$1.25
☐	THE WICKED MARQUIS	8467	$1.25
☐	LOVE IS INNOCENT	8505	$1.25
☐	THE FRIGHTENED BRIDE	8780	$1.25
☐	THE FLAME IS LOVE	8887	$1.25

Buy them at your local bookseller or use this handy coupon:

Bantam Books, Inc., Dept. BC, 414 East Golf Road, Des Plaines, Ill. 60016

Please send me the books I have checked above. I am enclosing $_____ (please add 35¢ to cover postage and handling). Send check or money order —no cash or C.O.D.'s please.

Mr/Mrs/Miss_____

Address_____

City_____State/Zip_____

BC1—9/76

Please allow three weeks for delivery. This offer expires 9/77.

Barbara Cartland

The world's bestselling author of romantic fiction. Her stories are always captivating tales of intrigue, adventure and love.

Bantam Book Catalog

It lists over a thousand money-saving best-sellers originally priced from $3.75 to $15.00 —bestsellers that are yours now for as little as 60¢ to $2.95!

The catalog gives you a great opportunity to build your own private library at huge savings!

So don't delay any longer—send us your name and address and 25¢ (to help defray postage and handling costs).